WAYWARD GODS

SOULS OF THE ROAD
BOOK FIVE

DEVON MONK

ODD
HOUSE
PRESS

For my family, the Ratties, and all the dreamers and wanderers on the road…

CHAPTER ONE

Lula hit the brakes, sending clouds of New Mexico dust over the top of the truck and through the open windows. It covered me, our dog Lorde sitting on the floorboard, and Abbi, who looked like an eight-year-old girl with white-blonde hair, but was actually the rabbit in the moon.

"What?" I leaned forward, the bench seat creaking under my weight, and scanned the rutted road we'd been following for nearly a hundred years.

"Those are wild asters, Brogan." Lu pointed at the scrubby purple and yellow wildflowers that bloomed everywhere along Route 66.

"Are they a problem?" I wasn't sure how a flower could be a problem, but we'd had plenty of strange happenings lately.

We'd battled vampires, fought ancient creatures, and made deals with demons and ghouls—some of whom insisted they were on our side.

The god Atë was hunting us, hunting us and the

spell book of the gods we'd hidden in the witch's box in the back of the truck. She wanted us dead so she could unlock its magic.

It was enough to make a man more than a little twitchy.

Lu huffed a laugh and shook her head. Her red hair was pulled back in a single braid, and freckles stood out against the pale skin of her face and arms.

"Not everything is a problem, Brogan." She left the door open and strolled out to pick the flowers.

"It could have been a problem," I muttered.

Lorde lifted her head, sniffing the air. The dog spotted the open door and took it as an invitation. She scrambled over my legs, all black fur and fluffy tail.

That left just me and Abbi in the truck. I stretched, savoring the extra space. The cab was a tight fit for all of us, especially since I was not a small man.

"I think she just likes flowers." Abbi patted her ruffled skirt, puffing more dust into the air, then waving it away from her face.

"I know she likes flowers. But why those? It's miles before we hit the end of the Route and try to leave it so we can drive that damned book to Oregon. Plenty more chances to pick flowers along the way."

"Maybe she's just happy to see them." Abbi's shadow, Hado, who took the form of a little black kitten, jumped from her shoulder to her lap and batted at her fingers. Abbi giggled. "Or maybe she's just happy."

I craned to get a better view of my wife.

Had Lula been smiling more the last few days? Since

we'd found the spell book of the gods and hidden it in the witch's box? Had it given her hope?

Hope for a life without angry gods on our tail who wanted us dead—or worse—wanted to use us to access the magic in the book?

Hope for a tomorrow where we didn't have to look over our shoulders for monsters and demons and betrayal?

Hope for life, just that—*life*—lived together?

Lu tucked a flower behind her ear and bent to pick more.

Abbi was right. She was smiling.

How had I missed that?

It wasn't like our troubles were over.

Still, Lula was happy.

And anything that made Lula, my love, happy, was everything I wanted too.

I swore under my breath, slid across the seat and put boots to dust. It was time to pick a few flowers.

And when Lula noticed, oh, the smile she gave me.

With our hands full of asters, we walked back to the truck.

Wildflowers were everywhere now, in Lu's hair, woven in a chain around her slender wrist, hanging bundled from the rearview mirror.

It was late morning and warm enough, I was trying not to nod off.

"It stinks here." Abbi wriggled, her elbows digging into my thigh and arm as she propped up on her knees.

I grunted.

She sniffed at the dashboard and the muggy air pushing through the vent. "Do you smell it? The stink?"

I yawned and brushed my fingers across Lula's bare shoulder, her skin a wonder of silk. I had spent too many years un-bodied as a spirit, unable to touch her, to not want to touch her now I was solid again.

Lu glanced over, a rise of eyebrow.

"I don't smell anything," I said. "Just New Mexico in September."

Abbi shifted, and Hado, currently sleeping across her shoulders, mewled.

Lorde, our black chow chow shepherd, propped her head on my knee.

I scrubbed behind her ear, and she made a happy growly sound.

"It's not New Mexico," Abbi said.

"It is," Lula said.

Route 66 meandered across yellow grassy plains dotted with lava rocks and short, sturdy juniper trees. Sandstone outcroppings scalloped the blue sky uninterrupted by clouds.

"I *know* where we are but the smell..." She sniffed and wrinkled her nose. "Something I don't like."

"Is it a healthy vegetable?" I asked.

Now the wrinkled nose was pointed my way.

"No, it's..."

A wall of darkness screamed across the horizon, rushing toward us with avalanche force.

"Hell," I said. "Lu—"

"—God!"

That was all the time we had.

CHAPTER TWO

The darkness grew impossibly large, swallowing the road, the land, the state, and us in one gulp.

Lu must have stopped the truck, slammed on the brakes. She must have killed the engine because I couldn't hear it, couldn't feel any motion.

We weren't driving. We couldn't be.

The darkness barreled past us, trapping us in a tunnel of black, a massive, endless undulating serpent.

I held my breath, fear so thick, I was drowning in it.

But we were still on the road. Still in the truck. We had to be.

"It's a god," Abbi whispered, turning her face into my side. She clutched a silent Hado in her arms, his eyes glowing gold.

I tightened my arm around her, searching for a break in the shifting darkness, a sign it would pass us by.

Dull light flickered in lightning tongues through the black, but there was no end to the dark.

I reached for Lula, and she reached for me, holding tight against the storm.

The darkness slowed, serpentine undulations curling tight, tighter.

And then—

—nothing.

Silence fell, heavy as the last breath before death.

My heart sledgehammered, each slow strike shaking my bones, my nerves, my skin.

"Oh no," Abbi squeaked as power—god power— filled the air.

Lu squeezed my hand.

Gods—or rather one god—was out there in that darkness.

Atë, the goddess of ruin and misery, who had created horrific monsters and sent them to tear our souls to shreds and rip our lives apart. Monsters who had turned Lula into a *thrawn* and me into an earthbound spirit.

Atë who wanted what we had—the spell book of the gods. She'd been hunting for it for years. She'd finally found it—and us—last month, killing me, and burying Lu beneath a house.

It had taken the intervention of two other gods— Death, who refused to reap my soul, and Cupid, who had fought Atë—for us to escape.

Atë wanted the spell book to destroy the world.

We weren't going to let her do that.

The darkness turned rancid. It stank of filth, of corruption, of jealousy gone to rot.

She was looking for us. Looking for the book. I could taste her rage like bitter syrup dripping down my throat.

I knew, as every prey did, that if we moved, if we breathed too hard, she would see us and rip out our throats.

Time ticked as slowly as my heartbeat, fear blowing each second out of shape.

Sweat gathered at the nape of my neck and ran between my shoulder blades, swamping my pits, and sticking my shirt to my skin.

Everything in me screamed to run.

But I knew running would only get us seen, targeted, dead.

An orange flame flared to life, Atë's power catching fire like a search light aimed into the void. It swept over the truck and beyond, scanning for what she wanted.

The book.

Our world flickered between darkness, orange fire, and darkness again, god power penetrating this strange space, looking for us.

Lu stared straight ahead, utterly still. But she wasn't prey frozen in fear, she was a killer searching for a killer.

I tugged her hand, just the smallest motion to tell her not to go out there, not to leave me, not to face the god on her own. Lu loosened her grip on my hand, every line set for attack.

Well, hell.

I squeezed her hand, then let up on the pressure.

If she was going to go fight the god, I'd fight the god right alongside her.

But the orange slowly faded from a blinding wildfire to a dim sunset.

Abbi mouthed one word over and over, a prayer against my shoulder: *"Please, please, please."*

Then a sweet, clear hum poured out around us, growing louder and louder.

Lula's eyes widened in panic, her pupils dilated.

The sound was not coming from the darkness. It was coming from the back of our truck.

"Shit," I breathed.

The spell book of the gods was ringing. The cursed, coveted, dangerous, powerful book we'd hidden in a witch's box had picked this moment to make itself known.

The witches in Texas said the box would hide the book from gods, devils, monsters, and beasts.

Yet it responded to Atë's search like a tuning fork.

We couldn't reach the book unless we got out of the truck, couldn't throw a blanket over it to dampen the sound, not that a blanket would work.

Not that anything would work.

The hum grew louder, and orange fire burned bright again, scanning the sky.

One of us had to shut the book up before Atë found it.

I reached for the door handle, but Lula grabbed my wrist, her hold punishing, anchoring me to her side.

Her eyes were an inferno of reflected fire. *No,* she mouthed.

Before I could argue her into letting me go, Abbi ducked under our clasped hands and pulled the handle.

"No!" Lu and I shouted at the same time.

I caught Abbi around the waist, but she was small, squirmy, and determined. She threw her weight into the door, forcing it open a crack.

Just enough to let Hado, the little black cat, now a shadow made of claws and teeth, slip out into the fire and darkness.

Abbi shut the door and pulled her mortar and pestle into her lap. She closed her eyes and inhaled.

Then she shimmered, becoming both the eight-year-old girl and the ancient, celestial rabbit in the moon. She stirred her pestle in the mortar, drawing the soft silver power up from the bowl. It spun like cotton candy, soft, subtle light growing to surround the truck.

She tapped the pestle on the mortar's rim and the humming stopped.

I twisted to look back at the witch's box. It was covered in shadow—Hado—who glittered with strands of silver. Abbi's power was smothering the box, silencing the book.

I didn't know how long she could hold that silence against a god. I didn't know how long it would take until Atë gave up looking for us.

I wrapped my arm around Abbi, holding her tight.

The orange fire exploded, a bomb detonating. If a color could scream, it was absolutely ear-shattering.

I squinted and hissed.

Then the light blinked out.

The temperature in the truck plunged, sudden arctic cold. I shivered, and tremors rattled through Lu and Abbi.

The book was still silent. Had Atë given up that quickly? Or had something else scared her away?

Sweat stung my eyes. I swallowed, the rot and bitterness of Atë's power coating my mouth.

Then the darkness moved, drifting as if a wind stretched and thinned it, becoming lighter and lighter until it was gray mist.

Abbi whispered, "A god."

At first, I thought she meant Atë. But then the mist cleared, until we were surrounded by clean yellow light.

There was no road. There was no land, horizon, or sky.

But there was a god.

He wore a long-sleeved linen tunic, loose trousers, and sandals made of strips of gold and turquoise. Layers of precious stones circled his neck, fanning out from shoulder to shoulder, the gold reflecting the light of the sun against his bronze skin and midnight hair.

Lu sneered.

We knew this god.

We'd been hounded by him before, nearly killed by him.

It had happened years ago, but not so long we would ever forget, or ever trust him again.

"Mithra," I growled.

"Broken souls." He flowed toward the truck, moving with impossible grace. "I've been looking for you."

CHAPTER THREE

"Drive," I said.

Lu put the truck in gear and gunned it.

The god grew large, larger but did not step aside.

The truck hit fifty, sixty, eighty miles an hour, but Mithra just smiled and opened his arms wide.

We were going to hit him. There was no avoiding a collision.

I shifted my hold on Abbi, pulling her against me and bracing my other arm on the ceiling of the cab.

Lu gripped the wheel and locked her elbows, bracing for impact.

Eighty, eighty-five miles an hour.

He was there, right there.

Lu yelled.

But there was no impact. We blew right through him.

All the light in the world went off, then snapped back on again.

We sat at a small outdoor café table, beside a quiet

city street. Large pots of flowers along the buildings and cobbled walkways sent heady fragrance into the soft breeze. Birds sang in lush green trees, and the low murmur of people around us filled the space.

The buildings, the language, the coffee set in front of us made me think we might be in France.

Well, not literally. Mithra was a god of contracts, of bindings. But that didn't mean he couldn't lie and cast an illusion if he wanted to.

I had to believe we were still in the truck, still on Route 66. I had to believe this god couldn't just snap his fingers and alter our reality so easily.

But he was a god. And gods could do anything.

"Brogan and Lula Gauge." He lifted his cup in a toast. "It has been some time since we last spoke."

"Since you tried to kill us," Lula snarled.

"That too." His smile was small and mean.

"The answer is no," I said.

"You don't even know what I am here to offer."

"The answer is still no."

"I don't like you," Abbi said.

Mitha's expression slipped from mostly human, to something cruel and bestial.

"You are insignificant to me." He snapped his fingers and Abbi turned into a small brown rabbit with one white foot.

She stood on her back feet and hopped, kicking the air.

Mithra snapped his fingers again.

Abbi froze as if he had just pressed a pause button.

"Let her go," I said.

"When I choose." He sipped his drink and inclined his head. "If I choose."

Have I mentioned how much I hated this guy?

Lorde, standing on the cobbles next to Lula, pressed her ears back and growled.

Mithra raised his hand, fingers ready to snap.

"Stop!" Lula grabbed Lorde's collar, and Lorde immediately sat. "We're listening," she said. "Talk."

Mithra's smug expression made me want to pop him in the nose just to see if he'd bleed.

He relaxed his hand and settled his cup onto the saucer. The liquid in it was not coffee. It was nebula fire that smelled of hot stone, burned copper, and ash.

"You may know I have been watching you."

"No," she said. "We didn't know."

"We don't care," I said.

"You should." He waved at our cups encouraging us to drink.

The liquid smelled strongly of coffee, rich and real. I wouldn't touch it with a ten-foot pole.

Lu pressed her palm on the table, her fingers so stiff, her knuckles were white. "Why were you watching us?"

"Because I see all contracts. You recently entered into a contract with a god. You bound yourself to him, even after you denied me the same."

"Again," I said, "you tried to kill us."

"You," he said to me, "I would have killed. You," he nodded at Lula, "I would have left exactly as you are. Why ruin a masterpiece?"

Pop him in the nose *and* punch him in the throat.

"Atë and her monsters turned you into powerful

tools that can find the spell book of gods, touch it, and unleash its power. It would have been better for…well, the mortal world at least…if I had killed you both.

"I was willing to take you off the chessboard…then. But now…now I think I might give you exactly what you most need to survive."

Lula and I exchanged a look. Was he gonna give us the same sales spiel every god, devil, and monster had rolled out over the years?

The old—*I see you have a problem, and I assure you, I am your only solution*—pitch?

I couldn't help it, I snorted.

"You think I won't kill you?" he asked.

Yes, he was a god of immense power. There was no questioning he could kill us if he wanted. But from the time and effort he was putting into convincing us he had the upper hand, that he had *the* solution to all our problems, told me just the opposite.

If he'd wanted to kill us, we'd have already been dead.

He wanted us alive.

Because he wanted something from us.

"No, go on. What are you planning to give us so we can survive?"

It must have been my tone, because his eyes narrowed.

I leaned back and crossed my arms over my chest, waiting.

"I am the god of contracts, rules, and justice. Any contract made can be unmade by me. *Any* contract."

If he was waiting for some kind of big reaction he didn't get it.

Lula shifted her grip on Lorde, encouraging her to lie down. "We know who you are." She sounded as bored as I did. "What's the offer?"

Again, the lines between his eyebrows showed his annoyance.

"I will release you from Atë's claim. I will break the contracts with which Cupid has bound your lives, your souls to him. I will break the deals you have made with the demon prince and that useless excuse of a trickster, Raven."

Time ticked. Lorde growled again, a low sustained warning. The people around us went on living their lives, as if we weren't even here, as if they couldn't see us.

In all likelihood, they couldn't.

I knew my answer. It was the same answer I'd always had for gods in general and this one god in specific.

Hell no.

I thought Lula would be on the same page, but she had surprised me in the past, so I looked to her.

"No," Lula said.

Okay, maybe we were on the exact same page.

Mithra didn't like being defied. But then, I'd never met a god who did.

"I don't offer this to you lightly," he warned.

"Light, heavy," I said, "the answer is still no."

He pulled his shoulders back and scowled.

"Perhaps you didn't hear me." Every word fell like a hammer striking concrete. "I have watched Atë manipulate you. I have watched her break and mold you into the instruments she needs to control the power in the spell book. She has *no* right to that power."

Lula's expression was fierce, but her voice was steady. "We agree. The book should not be in Atë's control."

He nodded like we were on our way to finally signing our lives over to him.

A pen appeared in his hand. It glinted with rare metals and stones bound with ribbons of stars.

"Give your lives to me," he ordered. "Relinquish the spell book into my care. You will be at my summoning if the book is to be accessed. You will cast the spells within it at my demand.

"In return, I will break the bonds Atë has placed upon you. I will break the contracts Cupid forced you into. I will put an end to the agreements, promises, and deals you have made with all monsters, devils, and demons.

"Give your souls to me and bow to my grace and rule."

Paper shimmered into existence, glowing on the table between us.

The city and people all seemed more distant as if we were leaving a dream behind us.

Birdsong silenced. The wind died. Colors drained to gray.

Mithra changed too. He was taller, grander, and unsettlingly alien in a way a human could never achieve. His power radiated a tempting perfume that I knew only masked endless corruption.

The look of determination on Lula's face was the same as mine.

We were going to fight another god, this god.

Again.

We had escaped him once, but I'd been a spirit and had more power to help Lula get away from him.

I wasn't a spirit now. We didn't have god-killing weapons. What did we have?

Lu had her knives hidden on her, because she always had her knives hidden on her.

I still had the vampire-killing knife Ricky had given me.

None of our knives would kill a god.

But we were about to find out if they would slow a god down.

I readied myself to hit him with everything I had, to give Lu and Abbi and Lorde as much time as possible to run.

To get free.

"We understand your offer," I said, leaning forward to rise, one hand reaching toward the pen (which I absolutely was not going to touch), the other curling around the hilt of the knife at my hip. "And our answer is no."

Mithra towered over us before I could register the motion. His power crackled with lightning.

"You dare…" he bellowed.

But I was moving, ignoring my instinct screaming that this was my death, this was my end.

I surged to my feet and rushed around the table, knife drawn to plunge in his throat.

Lula, faster than me, stronger than me, scooped up

Abbi, who was no longer frozen, and set her safely on the ground.

Then Lula didn't bother with dodging around the table. She threw herself over it, straight at the towering deity.

She was there, already there before me, her knives flashing.

I thought I saw movement at the corner of my eye.

Abbi drew up, a furious swirl of silver moonlight and blackness—a girl, a warrior in silver armor, a bunny, a girl again—magic lapping around her.

She disappeared, leaving us behind to fight this fight. But that didn't matter. Nothing mattered except—

—Lula, a blur of fury and anger—

—Mithra, untouched. The inhuman cruelty of his smile as he lifted one hand—

—Thunder splitting the sky in two, a roar so loud, I yelled and heard nothing—

"Stop!"

That voice was in my head, my soul, in the very air I breathed.

Even though my knife was a fraction away from Mithra's neck, even though Lula had plunged both her blades into his chest, we were frozen.

Luckily, so was Mithra.

"You have no authority here," the voice—Cupid's— said, his words dripping in rage that burned. "You have no power here."

The memory of Raven telling us Cupid had come to Earth in his god form to fight Atë, to free us from her when she'd kidnapped Lula and tried to kill me, flashed through my mind.

Raven had said when a god fought a god on Earth, it wasn't something that could be ignored. All gods would see it. And since most gods were secretive assholes, they avoided battles in this reality.

But we were on the brink of two massively powerful deities fighting to the death on this earthly plane.

Mithra stepped back.

Lula's blades slid free, bloodless. I still couldn't move, not even enough to reach for her hands.

Mithra took one, two steps away, while Cupid—

—massive as the universe, pure white wings spread to the sky, golden armor, golden bow in hand, a quiver of gold and lead arrows over one shoulder—

—stepped forward, beside us, then in front of us, protecting us from Mithra's power.

His presence was soothing, a dense forest shade against a punishing sun.

I could breathe again. I could move again.

I wrapped my arms around Lula, just as she grabbed for me.

"You dare challenge me?" Mithra roared. "Here, upon this earth?"

"Stand between me and those within my protection, and I will challenge you throughout all realities and existences, Mithra. Leave now, and our quarrel ends without your destruction."

"You may be old," Mithra said, "but the scales of justice are not in your favor, Cupid."

"Justice never misses its mark." Cupid lifted his bow. "And neither do I."

Mithra showed no emotion, but something about him changed. His power grew darker, heavier.

The panic was back, telling me to run, *now*.

I pulled Lula closer, bracing for the explosion.

Then…

…we were in the truck, canted onto the shoulder of the road, the black clouds of an old storm rumbling away across the distant New Mexico horizon.

"Brogan?" Lula reached for me as I reached for her, our hands (always) finding each other.

"I'm fine. You?"

She nodded. "Abbi?"

"I'm right here," Abbi said from outside my door. "I called him. I could see him, so I called him because we needed help. We needed a lot of help."

"Who?" Lula asked. "Who did you call, Abbi?"

"Me," Raven, the trickster god said, leaning into Lula's open window. "She called me."

CHAPTER FOUR

R aven had copper skin and short, spiky dark hair. He wore a forest-green T-shirt that said Blow Your Balls—Crow's Nest across the front with faded jeans that had holes in the thigh.

A glint of trouble in his eyes matched his sly smile.

"We really have to stop meeting like this," he said.

"What are you doing here?" I demanded.

A god. Another damn god. How many did we have to deal with in one day?

"I called him," Abbi said. "I told you, I called him. We were in trouble. And Raven likes me."

Raven shrugged. "I do like her."

"The hell?" The shock of Atë hunting us, of Mithra trapping us, of Cupid saving us, rolled through me, adrenalin and relief spiking. "*Why* did you call him?"

"Because he knew where I was." Cupid came into view and stood behind Abbi. He still wore his warrior god trappings—armor and wings and weapons and power.

"We don't need any more gods," I half-shouted.

Lu's hand landed on my arm. "These are better than some."

"*Most*," Raven said. "Better than most."

"We need to talk," Cupid said, all business. "Brogan, Lula, I'm going to take us somewhere safe where we won't be overheard."

"A real place?" Abbi asked. "On Earth? Near Route 66?"

"Yes," Cupid said. "Real and on Earth."

"If you want my opinion…" Raven said.

"I don't," Cupid said.

"The beach is beautiful this time of year," Raven went on, undeterred. "Oregon beaches in particular."

"Crow," Cupid warned.

Raven chuckled at the nickname. "Fine. Do it your way. But I'm coming, too, because I'm a part of this now whether you—"

"It's just caw-caw-caw." Cupid flicked his fingers, and we were (once again) no longer on the side of the New Mexico highway, though we were still inside the truck.

The trees, the sky, the dirt, all told me we were in Oklahoma.

So did the farmhouse set at the end of the winding path.

I'd been dropped off here by the god of death when I'd been killed by Atë, and Death had refused to let me cross to the other side.

Abbi had been waiting for me here. So had the owner of the house, Euterpe, the muse of music, poetry, and delight, who went by the name, Eunice Woodbury.

After we'd rescued Lula from where Atë had buried her beneath a house, this was where we'd sheltered to heal.

We'd also made our last deal with Cupid here.

I wondered if that was why he had brought us back —to renegotiate the deal.

"Oh," Raven said in a tone I'd never heard out of him before (I assumed it was respect). "Really, Bo? I didn't know you'd get her involved."

Cupid let out a deep breath. He no longer looked like a god with wings and gold armor.

He looked the way I remembered him first appearing to us months ago. Like an old biker, gray-bearded, bald, with diamonds in his ears.

His black leather vest revealed muscular arms tattooed with an intricate dove down his right forearm, and an owl down his left. The word "gold" was written across his right knuckles; "lead" was inked across his left.

Everyone assumed he was the god of making people fall in love, and I supposed that was true. But he was also a very old god—one of the oldest—if he were to be believed.

His power was both connection and destruction. From our short time knowing him, I had seen the destruction firsthand.

But he'd also given me back my solid form, here in this living world with Lula, in exchange for finding the spell book of the gods and helping people he thought needed help.

There was kindness in him, though I'd long ago given up on trusting gods.

"I didn't involve her, Raven," Cupid said. "Eunice involved herself."

Raven hummed. "I wonder why?"

"Go on and ask her. It seems there are a lot of meddling deities who want to be involved with the Gauges today. And with the spell book, *Crow*."

"I can't help but think you mean me," Raven said. "You do mean me, don't you? Interested in the Gauges who are, admittedly, interesting. And the spell book, the book I want wiped off the face of the universe? The book I hate more than I hate volunteering for a particular bossy Valkyrie? That book? It needs meddling in, don't you think, *Bo?*"

"I think we need to go." Cupid tapped a finger on the side view mirror. "She's expecting us."

"Will there be cake?" Abbi asked.

Cupid's smile was fond. "I'm certain she has something delicious cooked up. She knew we were coming."

Abbi's eyes grew large, once again a little girl excited for treats. She glanced toward the house and took a step, then stopped and looked back at us.

"I better go see if she's home." She took another step. "Just in case she needs help. With the cake. Or cookies. I'm a good helper." She turned and trotted up the path. "Hello! Are you home? Do you need help with a cake?"

Lorde woofed, and wagged her tail, watching Abbi go. She whined at the window, impatient to follow.

Lula pressed her lips together. I knew what she was

thinking: Were we going to just go along with the gods and moon rabbit, or were we going to run?

Frankly, I didn't think we'd get far if we decided to bolt.

"We should listen." I tipped my head toward Cupid. "We have some things to settle with him too."

Things like, we'd found the spell book of the gods and didn't want to hand it over to him as we'd promised. Things like we'd made a deal with a demon, and with Raven, to eventually take the book to Ordinary.

Lu opened the door. "A cup of tea sounds lovely." She slid out of the truck, her movements smooth and graceful. She didn't show any sign that she'd just faced down a god and buried her knives in his chest.

She looked calm and relaxed, like this was just a lazy late-summer day.

"Coming?" she asked.

As if she had to. Where she went, I went.

"So, this is fun." Raven strolled over to Cupid. "Want to clue me in on what exactly you're going to talk about?"

"Coffee first," Cupid said.

I opened my door and Lorde jumped out onto the grass. She sniffed at Cupid's boots and tipped her head up, panting happily.

Cupid scrubbed her head. "There's a good girl." He offered her a treat, which she took gently from his fingers before crunching and chewing.

"C'mon, Lorde!" Abbi called from the porch. "She has cake!"

Lorde woofed and galloped to catch Abbi, tail wagging.

Cupid started up the road after them, Raven matching his stride.

"You're so magnificent," Raven said. "Full battle armor. And those wings? Sparkle, sparkle."

"Shut up, Crow." Cupid punched him in the shoulder. Raven chortled.

"So manly and powerful. I think I'm in *love*."

Cupid took another swing but Raven, still laughing, sidestepped the blow.

I took Lu's hand, and she leaned into me before we followed everyone. Yes, we were leaving the spell book in the witch's box in the back of the truck.

So far, neither god had commented on it. I thought Hado might still be obscuring it from them.

"We said we'd give it to him," I said.

"I know," she whispered. "I don't think we should."

"I don't think we should either."

She looked up at me, and her eyes were golden, the sun drenching her heart-shaped face in soft light that made the freckles across her nose and cheeks stand out. I turned so I could cup her face with my other hand.

"I love you, Lula Gauge."

She smiled, and my heart beat faster. "I love you too, Brogan Gauge."

"We're here!" Abbi yelled. "Eunice? We're ready for cake!"

"Moon bunny!" Eunice's voice was melodious and happy. "I hope you like carrot spice cake. I have one with your name all over it."

"My name?" Abbi shouted in delight. "I love my name! Is there ice cream too?"

She darted into the house, Lorde on her heels.

Eunice, who I'd always thought of as the Owl Woman, looked much the same as the last time I'd seen her.

More crone than matron, her white hair bunched and puffed around her round face like carded wool. She wore layers and layers of autumn-colored skirts, blouse, and vest, with a green crocheted shawl draped over her shoulders to top it all off.

Her wrists and ankles were decorated with beads and charms which chimed and rattled as she moved, all the world leaning in to listen to her music.

"Raven, Cupid," she said as they reached the porch, "come on in. Coffee's hot and there's tea."

They both paused to give her a hug before walking over the threshold.

She waited until Lula and I stepped onto her porch.

"Lula," she said, "Brogan. I am so pleased you're here. There were many futures and for a time…" She shook her head. "…For a time I didn't think you'd be stopping by. Come on in. We have decisions to make. Time isn't on our side. Not enough of it, anyway."

She placed her hand on each of our shoulders, and the acceptance and friendship in her touch was the warmest welcome.

"I hope we're not bringing too much trouble to your doorstep with us," Lu said.

Eunice grinned, showing the gap in her teeth, the

wrinkles on her face fanning at the edges of her eyes and cupping under her knobby cheeks.

She leaned forward. "Oh, you are, you very much are bringing trouble. But I wouldn't have it any other way. What was it Cupid said just a moment ago? I have *involved* myself in these matters, along with all manner of deities."

She stepped back to give us room, and then we were in her house, which smelled of sweet spices and browned butter—through the front room, and into her kitchen.

Once in the kitchen, Lu took a deep breath, and the tension she'd been hiding drained out of her.

I felt the same. Being in the heart of the Muse's home was the safest I'd felt in a long time.

Abbi sat on her knees in a chair and was cutting a large slice of carrot cake with an equally large knife. Cupid and Raven huddled at the coffee pot, pouring mugs while talking quietly in a language that slid away from my mind and left no impression.

Lorde had settled into a soft bed on the floor and was happily chewing on a bone.

"There's tea." Eunice gestured toward the kettle and little flowered canisters with hand-written labels on them. "Brogan, I've got cold chicken in the fridge and a fresh loaf of sourdough if you want a sandwich."

I hadn't thought I was hungry, but as soon as she said it, my stomach rumbled. I was starving.

"Lu?" I cut off toward the fridge. "Food?"

"I'll start with tea."

We moved about the kitchen, Eunice setting out

plates and Abbi cutting more reasonably sized pieces of cake for everyone.

By the time I came to the table with my sandwich, she'd already wolfed through two huge slices of cake.

I took the knife away before she could cut herself a third.

"Hado wants some!" she said.

"Hado isn't in the kitchen, is he?"

She wrinkled her nose, her gaze searching for the meaning in my words. "Hado's in the truck. He wants to stay in the truck. Because he's tired."

"Good." Hado was still guarding the book. "He should get some rest. We'll give him cake later. If you don't eat it all first."

"It has my name on it. I *should* eat it all."

I dropped a half sandwich on her plate and pointed at it.

She gave me a brief scowl, then dug in, humming a song about the moon and pizza pies as she chewed.

"Well then." Eunice joined us, a huge mug of tea in her hands. "I'm glad to see you all made it. What are we going to do about Atë and that damnable book?"

Raven and Cupid turned and stared at us expectantly.

Lula sipped tea, as if it didn't bother her to be the subject of that much god attention. I settled into my chair, squaring off with my own sandwich.

"I'm open to suggestions," I said.

"We need a plan." Cupid took the chair at the head of the table opposite Abbi. "And we should execute it before she and Mithra can pull another stunt like that again."

"Mithra," Eunice said. "I'd wondered." She shook her head. "All right then. What do we do about them?"

"If you want my opinion—" Raven offered.

"We don't," Cupid said.

Raven huffed and leaned against the counter. "Just wait, you will."

"The gods are only part of the problem," Cupid said. "The spell book is its own challenge."

"We have it," Lula said, "the book. But you knew that, didn't you?" Her golden gaze shot up to meet Cupid's. Fearless, that woman. Standing her ground against monsters, fate, and the gods themselves.

I couldn't help but throw her a grin.

Cupid linked his fingers on top of the table. "The hunter gave it to you."

"Did you see us?" Abbi asked. "Did you see me melt the vampires and save us?"

"I saw the book being moved by the hunter, and I saw you find it in Texas."

"Boo," Abbi said, "you missed the best part. The part where I was bright as the *sun* and saved us."

"Is that why you brought us here?" I asked. "You want us to give you the book?"

Cupid didn't move, but there was more god to him now, a darkness and power barely contained behind his guise of humanity.

"Is that our agreement, Brogan Gauge?" It was a warning, a challenge—pure god stuff.

But like Lula, I wasn't inclined to back down. "You told us to bring it to you when we found it."

"Which you have done. I am here. You are here. The book is in the truck."

"No fair!" Abbi said. "You can see it?"

"Not now. Hado and the witch's box are cloaking it. But for those few moments in Texas when it was not in the witch's box, Atë and Mithra must have sensed it near you. I saw it."

"So, they know." Lula glanced out the window, as if the other gods were headed our way.

"If they'd known it was in the truck," Raven reasoned, "they would have taken your truck and disposed of both of you."

"They can't touch it though," Eunice said. "They need Lula and Brogan to access the spells. There's no using the book without them."

Raven tucked his hands into his front pockets, shoulders back, head tipped. He looked relaxed, but it was the kind of pose a hawk would take before striking.

"They don't need them alive," he said. "Brogan's better to them as an unbodied spirit. When he's nothing but a ghost, they can better control Lula."

Lu tucked her hair behind her ears and narrowed her eyes at Cupid. "Are you taking the book from us?"

"No. That wasn't our agreement. I'm asking what you want to do with it."

Eunice made a little noise of surprise. "Excuse me a minute. I'll be back in a nip." She walked out of the kitchen.

A second later, Hado in black kitten form, bounded into the room and jumped up on Abbi's lap.

He hissed at Cupid, his ears back.

"It's okay," Abbi said. "You did a good job. The bad gods didn't get it, did they?"

Hado's ears flicked back up, he *mew*ed, and bumped his head on Abbi's stomach. She smiled and stroked his back.

"I know what I want you to do with it." Raven sat at the table. The air took on a weight, a feeling of fate, of momentous decisions about to be made.

I hated that feeling.

"I want the book in Ordinary. Sandy beaches, mild weather, lots of weird—I mean quaint—small town festivals. The magical library can disappear powerful books from gods, monsters, and anything else in this earthly realm."

"You're not the one making the choices here," Cupid said. "They are. Brogan, Lula?"

This was it, then. Our chance to defy Cupid. To change, once again, our agreement with him—the agreement which had brought me back to life and given us his protection.

"We won't give it to you," I said, "or any other god."

Lula lifted her chin, gaze steady. Her hand slipped down to the knives hidden on her.

"Free will," Raven said. "I told you."

"Free will." Cupid took a long breath and sat back.

The tension in the room broke like sunlight through fog.

"Did you change your mind?" Raven asked. "Are you going to keep it?"

"Do we have to tell you what we want to do with the book?" I asked.

"Everything is an option." Eunice strode into the room, bracelets chiming. "Free will, like these two just said." She checked the refrigerator for cream, then pulled out a bowl, sugar, and a mixer.

"We're taking it to Ordinary." Lula nodded. "To the secret library there."

I'd never seen two gods and a muse smile the same smile of relief.

"Agreed," Cupid said. "It belongs in Ordinary."

"Ah-ha!" Raven crowed.

"But," Cupid continued, "there is something you need to know which might change your mind about that."

Raven groaned. "Are we doing this now?"

"They deserve the truth," Cupid said.

Eunice turned on the mixer, and the scent of vanilla filled the air. Whipped cream, I thought.

Raven spread his hands, giving Cupid the floor.

"I found the monster who attacked you," Cupid said.

The world went oddly slick and distant, as if nothing about it was quite real. A ringing filled my ears.

Shock, I thought.

"There is only one still alive, but I have found him."

This is what we'd been looking for, what Lula and I had spent all these years hunting.

The monster who had torn our souls apart, taken

our lives and locked us into following Route 66, the magical pathway that had carried supernaturals and monsters across the United States for a hundred years.

"Where?" I asked.

"Who?" Lula asked.

Cupid's fingers tapped the tabletop as he looked between us.

"You've been working with him for years. Lula, you collected magical items for him."

"No," I breathed, knocked back by the horror of it, the injustice of it.

"Headwaters?" Lula growled.

"Headwaters," Cupid agreed.

CHAPTER FIVE

L ula stood so quickly, she was a blur. She drew her lips back in a snarl, her hands in fists. She was wrath, she was hellfire.

"How long?" she demanded. "How long have you known it was Headwaters?"

"Not long," Cupid said. "Only after my battle with Atë."

"Weeks?" she growled. "You waited weeks to tell me?"

"Lu," I warned.

She couldn't hear me, deafened by the rage, the helplessness, the hunger for revenge. We'd spent a hundred years longing to kill the creature who had done nothing but cause us pain.

To find out the same creature had been toying with us all these years was infuriating.

"I waited," Cupid said, "because if you kill Headwaters—which I know you want to do—it will kill you. You and Brogan, both."

"That—what?" I spun toward Cupid. "How?"

Lula took a step back from the table, clumsy, blinded by hatred, the back of her legs knocking over the chair.

"Don't," she hissed at him. "Don't you *dare* take this from me."

"Lu." I reached for her. "Love."

But she couldn't see me. Not through the outrage. Not through the memories. Not through the pain.

She shook her head and stormed out of the room, every inch of her brittle with anger.

I took a step, but Hado *mew*ed, jumped off Abbi's lap, and trotted after her.

"Give her time," Eunice said, scooping the whipped cream into a smaller bowl. "She's safe here. She won't leave you behind."

I wasn't so sure. She had made decisions to leave me behind before. I started toward the door, but Abbi slipped her hand into mine.

"Hado will tell me if anything happens." Her eyes were huge and pleading, holding all of the galaxy's stars like rivers of light. "We need answers, right?"

I scrubbed my other hand over my face.

I hated this. All of it. I didn't know what our future might be—if we would even have a future beyond killing Headwaters and getting rid of the book—but if I had any say, our future would be far, far away from monsters and gods.

"All right," I said. "Talk. Where's Headwaters?" I didn't sound as furious as Lula, but it was close.

Cupid sighed. "If I tell you, you're going to leave right now to kill him, aren't you?"

"The thought crossed my mind."

"You can't kill him yet. Brogan…" He looked away and rubbed the top of his bald head. "Anger will warm you, but only cold logic will save you. You and Lula."

"Cold logic and a weapon you don't know how to wield," Raven said.

Cupid threw Raven a look, and Raven held up his hands. "I'm not wrong."

"He's not wrong." Eunice's voice was melody and harmony, a chorus of her power centering upon this moment, stitching us into this reality, this now.

I paced to the windows at the back of the kitchen that overlooked Eunice's property.

Lula was walking through the field, the summer grass yellowed and gone to seed. She wasn't alone. A little black cat hopped along beside her, and overhead, three crows swooped and circled.

She hadn't left. She hadn't left me yet.

"What weapon?" I asked, gathering what calm I could. "Tell me what weapon kills Headwaters."

"There's probably more than one," Cupid said. "But to kill it…completely…you will need to use the spell book of the gods."

Everything went silent. I almost expected a flash of lightning or a blast of storm wind to roll through the house.

But there was just the soft ticking of a clock in the other room and the call and reply of the crows—Raven's crows, undoubtedly—outside against the faded blue sky.

"First you want us to find the book, then hand it

over, then hide it, and now you want us to use it? How many more roles are we going to play in this game, Cupid?"

"I don't want you to use the book. I don't want anyone to use it. But I can't make that choice, because, as we've just illustrated, you and Lula have free will, Brogan Gauge."

Raven grunted. "We really should have given mortals something else in exchange for their worship."

"Don't start with that," Cupid said. "You wanted them to have free will."

"Well, it is fun, isn't it? More interesting too."

"How," I asked, "can we use the book to kill him?"

"There should be spells in the book…" Cupid raised an eyebrow, and Raven nodded. "There *are* spells in the book made by powerful beings who have left this reality, and essentially no longer exist."

"Lost gods," Eunice said, surprised.

"We don't speak of them, much," Raven mused. "But then, we didn't speak of the book for so many centuries everyone forgot about it."

"Not everyone," Eunice said.

Raven pointed at her in agreement.

"Do the lost gods know about me and Lula?"

"I fucking hope not," Cupid said. "Those gods are no longer connected to Earth, to this plain of existence, but the spells they left in the book? It's possible the spells they left behind can be used without the dire consequences of the other spells."

"Magic without a price?" I asked.

"No, there could still be a price," Cupid said. "Will likely be one. But not your death. Not Lula's death."

"The spells will protect them?" Eunice asked.

"Not protect," Raven said. "They just won't carry the backlash and repercussions—death, destruction, shackled worship—of tapping into the spell of a living god." He lifted his mug up to Cupid. "That's a very sneaky loophole. I didn't think you had it in you, Bo. I approve."

Cupid's smile spread slowly, giving him a wolfish look. "You agree?"

"That a wayward god's spell might kill Headwaters without Lula or Brogan paying for it with their lives? Yes. In theory. We won't really know until they try, which is its own problem. And as soon as they tap the book, it's gonna draw attention."

"I know of a place that could keep them hidden. With people who will look out for them," Eunice said. "I think…" She hummed and tapped a beat I could not hear against her thigh. "So many possibilities."

I did not want to use that damned book. Just because a spell might not kill us, didn't mean the price wouldn't be higher than we wanted to pay.

There were worse things than death.

"Let me guess," I said. "This place where we can use the book without Atë or other gods finding us is Ordinary."

Eunice put her hands on her hips and shook her head. "Ah-yah. Are you so ready to believe the worst of me, Brogan Gauge? We are here to see that you and

Lula survive. We are here to see the book put to rest. Even Raven has good intentions."

"Hey now," Raven said. "Don't go ruining my reputation. Trickster god, remember?"

"Oh, you've plenty of tricks, but not against the Gauges. You hate that book more than any of us. Why, you're here in my kitchen, breaking a promise to the Reed sisters, to see that it is buried for good."

"My promise to Delaney isn't broken, it's just…flexible. My hatred for that book, is not." There was so much god power behind those last words, I tasted ash in my mouth.

"You know I will bend my power to keep you safe and hidden," Cupid said.

"Safe? Like when Atë almost killed me and buried Lu? Or when Lu almost died fighting the king vampire? Were you keeping us safe when the Hush swarmed us? When Lorde was shot?"

Cupid tipped his head.

Out in the field, Lula stood very still, her shoulders angled toward me. Her supernatural hearing caught every word, even though she was several yards away from the house.

"No," Cupid said. "I have not kept you safe or hidden. You were within my awareness, but my protection was slow. Until I fought Atë."

"After she'd tried to kill me. *After* she'd kidnapped Lu."

He inclined his head. "I didn't expect her direct approach. I did not expect her at all."

"Time is long, Brogan," Raven said. "Even the most powerful gods become forgetful."

It sounded like an omen, like a line from a very old poem.

It sounded like the truth.

"I will keep you hidden from Atë," Cupid said. "I will keep you hidden from Headwaters. I am giving you time to learn how to use the spells of the lost gods, if that is what you choose to do."

"What if we find another weapon to kill Headwaters?"

"If that is your choice, I will keep you hidden and protected to the extent of my powers for however long— months, years, decades—it will take to find that weapon. But you have made enemies of gods. There are ways they could make you suffer that even I cannot save you from."

"Damned if we do," I said.

He made a considering sound.

"Can you guarantee the price we pay for wielding lost god magic won't be too steep?" I asked.

"Define steep," Raven said.

"That either of us dies. That we lose our humanity, our souls, our minds. That we will come out of it so changed we are no longer capable of loving each other. Of being who we are."

"Your souls," Cupid drew on his god power, putting intent behind it, "are always yours. Unchangeable. Perfect. Free."

"But," Raven added.

Cupid glared at him.

"They need to know, Bo. If they're going to agree to this. If they are going to use the blasted book and take it to its final resting place, they need to know it all."

Cupid tapped his finger on the table again. He stared into a middle distance, seeing things I could never —would never—care to see.

Lula shifted, turning so she was in profile. The sun poured over her like honey, making her pale skin glow and her red hair catch fire. Some of the fury had drained from her, but that didn't mean she wasn't angry.

She lowered her hand, and Hado bumped his head on her palm, then jumped to her. She caught him and held him at eye level, the two of them staring at each other for a long moment.

I didn't think she could talk to the moon rabbit's shadow, but maybe she could.

Maybe he was telling her we didn't have to do this. Didn't have to risk everything on a plan the gods had decided for us.

Free will, right?

Lula drew Hado closer and bent her forehead, touching her head to his.

I felt my heart clutch at the unbearably sweet moment.

She'd wanted children. I remembered that now. Back when we'd both been alive, before the attack, when the world wasn't so much an easier place as we were much, much more naive, she had whispered to me, on a summer's evening, that she liked children and hoped one day to have some.

She bent, and Hado jumped down into the tall grass next to her.

The moment, the memory, whisked away, leaving behind an unfamiliar longing for a tomorrow we might never have.

"What do we need to know?" I asked Raven.

Lula strolled back to the house. She couldn't see me looking at her through the window, not with the sun's angle on the glass. Still, her gaze was locked on mine.

I smiled, because there was nothing she didn't know about me. Nothing about her I didn't adore.

We were going to do this, kill Headwaters. We were going to use that damned book to do it.

I could see her decision in her stride, see it in the wild wind swirling around her.

We were going to take that monster down, no matter the price.

"You tell him or I do," Raven said.

Cupid sighed. "It's the spells. When you use the spells written by the lost gods, you may resurrect the lost gods from whatever reality they inhabit."

"And," Raven encouraged.

"And," Cupid crossed his arms over his chest, "they may not be pleased about it."

I raised my eyebrows, and Lula flashed a smile in return.

I didn't like this. I didn't want to touch the damn book, didn't want to use any spell in the damn book, didn't want to use god magic or lost god magic.

But however much I didn't want to use the book, I knew Lula wanted to kill Headwaters twice as much.

"Wait," Eunice said. "We have company."

"Here?" Raven asked. "Who?"

Eunice was already out of the kitchen, a wave of her hand dismissing the question.

Cupid and Raven exchanged a look, then did something with their power that made my molars hurt.

They were still sitting at the table, but they looked different in a way I couldn't put my finger on.

"Shhh…" Raven said. "We're in disguise. Don't want to startle the normals."

Voices rose at Eunice's door. A woman, no, more than one, and an older man's voice, all of them talking over each other like they were trying to explain the same thing, but were just making it impossible to understand.

"He's in the kitchen," Eunice said. "Lula's coming in from the field."

"Thank you very much, Ma'am," the man said. "We won't be long or too much trouble."

I knew that voice, but it didn't make any sense.

"Elmer?" I asked, just as the monster hunter, his granddaughter and her partner walked into the kitchen, guns on their hips.

CHAPTER SIX

"Been looking for you, Brogan." Elmer was an old man, his hair gone white and wispy, his ears liver spotted. But his eyes were sharp, and like most old monster hunters, there was strength in his body which spoke of a life spent working hard.

"There's important matters we need to discuss with you, private matters." He glanced at the gods at the table. "Now would be best. Gentlemen. No offense." He pointed toward the front door, and I had the impression he would have crossed the kitchen and grabbed me by the collar if he thought it would make me move faster.

"Wait now," Eunice said. "Coffee's still hot. I have pie and fresh whipped cream. Let's all sit down together."

"Plenty of room." Cupid scooted his chair to one side.

Elmer reconsidered Cupid and Raven, sharp gaze missing nothing. The gods might have tried to hide their power, but a life hunting dangerous monsters and para-normals had honed Elmer's instincts.

He had a good sense for hinky, and I could tell the alarm bells were going off.

"Brogan. You come on outside with me, now." Elmer backed toward the kitchen doorway where his granddaughter Pamela and her partner Josie lingered, their smiles now hard and wary.

They knew something was up too.

"We're not human," Raven said like he was discussing neighborhood gossip. "But we're friends of Brogan and Lula just like you, and we want them safe, just like you."

"Pamela, Josie, Elmer." Lula opened the kitchen door and stepped into the room, quiet, even in her boots. "Raven's right. They're friends."

"And they're not human," I added, shifting my stance to lean a shoulder against the wall.

"And her?" Elmer jabbed a thumb toward Eunice, who laughed.

"I like you," she said. "You're suspicious. I'm just Eunice nowadays. Back in the times, I was known as Euterpe. Muse of music." She made a little flourish with her hand, her bracelets jangling.

If Elmer had been wearing a hat, he would have snatched it off his head to hold it in front of him apologetically. Instead, he gave her a short bow. "I am pleased to meet you, ma'am. Sorry for barging into your house like this, but there are matters—timely matters—that can't be ignored."

"Headwaters?" Lula asked.

Pamela and Josie finally walked into the room. They each gave me a nod and a small wave which I returned. Even though they were less wary, I could tell they were not comfortable.

Whether it was from the news they had to share with us, or because they were in the company of power, I didn't know.

Pamela was lighter skinned, like her grandfather, her usually happy face round with a sharp chin, her brown hair cut in a sensible bob. She assessed the situation, then pulled out a chair and sat. "I bet your story is interesting," she said to Raven and Cupid. "Stand down, Grandpa. There's so much power in this room, we were outclassed before we even got through the door."

"You said pie, Eunice?" Josie had a darker complexion, her thick black hair held back with a kerchief, her delicate features and hazel eyes lending her beauty queen status.

"Cake, too," Eunice said, "but you all look like a cherry pie wouldn't be amiss."

"I prefer sour cherry, if it's not too much problem?" Elmer asked.

"Look at that!" Eunice said. "It just *happens* to be sour cherry. Coffee's by the window, cups to the left. Help yourself while I serve it up."

Elmer gave me one last look, hoping, I supposed, that I'd overrule everyone (and their quest for pie) to get us out of here quick.

Lula brushed her fingers across the back of my hand as she moved toward the coffee. I captured her fingers and knew we were okay. We were together on this, set on this road once again. Then she kept walking, and our hands slipped apart.

"I'll get the coffee," she said. "Go ahead and sit, Josie. Abbi, can you scoot over?"

"I'm gonna go outside and run!" Abbi said. "Hi, Pamela. Hi, Josie! Hi, Elmer! I ate cake. So much cake. It had my name all over it!" She hopped off the chair, grabbed Elmer in a fast hug and darted out of the room. "C'mon Hado! I want to chase bugs!"

Hado popped out from under the cupboard and galloped after her.

Elmer sighed and eased down into a seat next to Cupid. "Not human you say?" he asked Raven.

"Not in the least," Raven said. "Bo here stumbled on the Gauges a couple months ago."

"Stumbled?" Cupid shook his head. "I became aware of them when they unearthed the spell book of the gods. Which they lost."

"And found." Lula placed cups in front of Elmer, Pamela, and Josie, then leaned on the wall next to me.

I extended my arm, and she tucked into my side, my arm over her shoulder.

"You have some claim to that book?" Elmer asked Cupid.

"Not in the way you think."

Eunice dealt out plates filled with hearty slices of cherry pie.

"Whipped cream here if you want it." She placed the bowl and an earthenware crock in the middle of the table. "This is ice cream, if you'd rather. Now then, I've done my part. I'm going to go out and chase bugs with the moon rabbit. Hunters, you are welcome in my home. Gauges, listen to all the choices. I know you'll make the right one."

She hummed a song about skies and mountains and wandering streams, her voice sweet and hopeful as she rambled through the house, to open and shut the front door.

Elmer cut a bite of pie and chewed. He stopped, unruly eyebrows ticking upward, then pointed at his granddaughter. "Remind me to ask her for the recipe."

"Oh, it's that good, is it?" Pamela took a bite and swore under her breath. "That's amazing."

"Wait until you try the ice cream," Josie said.

It was good to see them enjoying food, strange to see them sitting next to gods, and stranger still that Raven and Cupid hadn't left yet.

"So, what's your claim to the book, then?" Elmer asked, eyes on his pie. "Since we're all friends here."

He didn't trust Cupid or Raven.

He was a very suspicious man.

I liked that about him.

"We have the book," I said. "We're looking for a place to hole up so we can see what it can do. Or what we can do with it."

I still didn't want to use the book and was going to do everything I could to talk Lula out of it. But if we had a hideout, we could search for some other weapon to kill Headwaters.

Elmer pointed his fork at Cupid and Raven. "And these two?"

"I am someone who wants the book out of everyone's hands," Cupid said. "My stake in this is to make sure no one can ever access it again."

"You?" Elmer asked Raven.

"Samesies. For my own reasons, but I want the same outcome. It needs to be hidden away. Locked up."

"Hidden things are always found again," Pamela said.

Josie hummed in agreement. "Can it be destroyed?"

Weirdly, Raven and Cupid looked at each other for the answer.

"Not that we know of," Raven finally said.

"Not that *anyone* knows of," Cupid corrected. "It's old and unique. The only relic of its kind. If there is a power that can destroy it, it likely would have done so by now."

"Probably," Raven said. "Enough people and powers have been looking for it. If it could have been destroyed someone would have done it."

"You don't think Brogan and Lula can destroy it, do you?" Pamela asked.

Cupid shrugged. "Maybe. But only Brogan and Lula will know."

All eyes turned our way.

"We don't know," Lula said. "We just got possession of it again. We haven't touched it to find out."

"Why's that?" Elmer asked.

"Because when we touch it," I said, "when *Lula* touches it, it's likely other things, other monsters and gods, will notice."

"And?" Josie asked.

"And head our way to kill us for the book."

"This doesn't make sense." Pamela sipped coffee, frown lines between her eyebrows. "These two are fine with you having the book even though they are obviously very powerful. No, I don't know exactly what you are, but I can see you're hiding a lot of power."

"Fair," Raven said.

"Why not take the book for yourselves?"

"Because we can't touch it," Cupid said. "Just as none of you can touch it. The book chooses who can wield the power within it. As far as I can tell, there are only two souls alive on Earth who can touch the book and cast its spells."

The eyes returned to us, this time with a mix of shock and worry.

"Hard luck," Elmer said. "You never want to be the chosen one in these sorts of situations."

"Don't we know it," I said.

"Then you really do need to hear why we drove three states to get to you," Elmer said. "You have a god on your tail."

"Mithra?" Lula asked. "Atë?"

"Not them," Pamela said. "The stirring on hunter radio—"

"—it's not an actual radio. Just a way we get important information to each other," Josie said. "Big information."

"Right," Pamela said. "We're hearing—everyone is hearing—that you're being hunted. By a god."

We were the target of another god. It should worry me, but we'd caught the attention of Cupid, Raven, and Death himself. We'd been hunted by Mithra, and Atë.

That was a lot of gods for one life.

It wasn't that I wasn't concerned, but the hits kept coming and nothing could surprise me right now.

What was one more god added to the pile of gods who were already trying to kill us?

"Who?" I asked. "Which god?"

"Apep," Elmer said. "The god who wants to destroy all creation."

CHAPTER SEVEN

"Oh, for fucks," Raven said. "Apep? That asshole? Like this couldn't get worse."

"Are you sure?" Cupid asked. "Elmer, are you very sure?"

"As can be." He scraped fork tines over the plate, catching the last of the red cherry glaze. "We've had multiple sightings, and at least one hunter asked the god his name, and he said Apep."

Raven took a last gulp of coffee. "I'll stay to the road," he said. "Do what I can to keep him off their trail. You taking on the big jobs, Bo?"

Cupid stood. "Yes. If I can pull him off this plane of existence, it should buy us some time. Lu, Brogan, you need to leave, now. I thought you had time to learn how to use the book, but there's no guarantee."

"Where?" I asked. "Where won't any of these gods find us?"

"Ordinary?" Lula asked.

"They'd know you were there," Raven said. "And

I'm not sure Delaney would allow you to use the book and cast god spells. We've recently had a run in with one page of the book. She's not a fan."

"Ricky's?" I asked Lu.

"Maybe?"

"No," Cupid said, as he and Raven moved toward the door. "The Crossroads is a beacon. You don't want to go there. Somewhere hidden. Somewhere," here he turned and looked straight at Elmer, "built to be safe."

"I have no idea what you're talking about." Elmer stood too. "That's it then. Let's get you out of here."

Eunice walked back into the room, Abbi right behind her with Hado in her arms.

"Which disaster is it?" Eunice asked. "The god?"

"The god," Raven said. "Thank you for your hospitality." He gave Eunice a hug and kissed her temple. "Stay safe." He spun and pointed back at us. "Don't forget Ordinary."

He turned, took a step, and was no longer a man. Instead, a single black raven with gold-tipped wings called out a rough song and flew up and up to disappear through the ceiling.

Cupid put one hand on Eunice's shoulder. He didn't say anything, and neither did she, but I could tell they exchanged information.

"Safe travels to you," she said. "I'll do what I can from here."

"You are under my protection, Lula and Brogan Gauge," he said, the power of the words warming like a fire against winter. "Nothing changes that."

He strode out of the kitchen and disappeared. A clap of thunder rolled in the cloudless sky.

"All right then," Eunice clapped her hands softly like a teacher asking for the class's attention. "You are being hunted by a very angry, evil god—more than one. You must leave and quickly. Elmer Walch and family, will you guide them to a place where they can learn to wield the spells in the book?"

"That's what we came here for," Pamela said. "Right, Grandpa?"

He frowned. I don't know what he saw in Lula and me, standing side-by-side, my arm over her shoulders, neither of us panicking over something that was undeniably panic worthy.

"Well, hell," he said. "Yes. We came here to tell you about the god, and to ask you if you needed a safe place to hole up."

Lightning flashed and thunder cracked, then rolled across the sky. A murder of crows called out, the shadow of wings passing over the window dappling the late afternoon sunlight.

"We need to go." Abbi darted over. "Brogan, we *really* need to go." Her eyes were huge, moonlight pooling in static blue.

A wind rattled the roof as if warning us to run, to fly, to drive as fast as we could away from the darkness hounding down from the horizon.

"Go," I said, putting my hand on Abbi's shoulder and urging her forward. "Get in the truck with Lorde and Hado."

"How far?" Lula asked Elmer.

We were all moving now, the wind heaving at the walls of the house, windows rattling.

Eunice shoved a canvas bag at Pamela as she passed by, and another bag, that looked like it held food, at Josie.

"It's out aways. New Mexico. Seven, eight hours if we drive fast," Elmer said.

"Then let's drive fast," I said.

Elmer stopped in front of Eunice. "Ma'am. Thank you so much for your hospitality. That pie was the best I've had in years. If you ever need a thing me or my family can assist with, you let us know."

She grinned, and it made her look years younger. "Thank you, Elmer. I appreciate you being here. This was…good timing."

Another flash of light and boom of thunder drowned out his reply. He glanced my way and pointed at the living room, indicating we should follow him.

"Eunice," I said.

"No time, Brogan Gauge. You need to run. And run now!"

Her voice carried the power of song, of fate, of realities strung together to make a chord, a symphony which thrummed down my spine and pushed me to move, to hurry, to run.

Lula took hold of my hand.

We ran.

Through the house, through the open door.

The sky was wide and wild, a mountainous wall of storm clouds churning on the horizon and swallowing the land.

Lightning licked blue and green, thunder exploded.

A spatter of rain, driven by the whipping wind struck my face, my arms, my head like sharpened nails.

We ran.

Elmer ducked into the back of Pamela's SUV, slamming the door just as the rain picked up.

Our truck, Silver, was close enough I could see Abbi sitting up on her knees in the cab, Lorde on one side, Hado on the other. But it felt like it was miles away.

The sky cracked open, and rain came down with a vengeance.

We ran.

I couldn't see the truck. Rain stung my eyes, blinding me, battering every inch of exposed skin.

It was cold—far too cold for Oklahoma—a blizzard of icy teeth biting and bruising. I held on to Lu and barged forward, my other hand stretched out, like I was going to tackle an oncoming football player.

My hand slapped the window of the truck. The driver's side.

Lula pulled away and wrested the door open, slipping inside.

I dragged my hand across the hood and staggered to the other side.

The wind howled—the sound of a wounded animal baring its fangs, ready to attack.

I yanked on the door, but it wouldn't open. Abbi lunged for the handle, pushing as I pulled.

The howling was closer, the wind made of wolves, of teeth—cold, alien, and hungry.

I yelled and pulled with everything I had.

The door swung.

I stumbled back and fell, knocking my head on the hard ground. I swore, dazed, and rolled onto hands and knees as the world swung and rocked. I pushed up to my feet.

The truck was just ahead, the door still open. I had to get into it.

I grabbed the frame of the door and swung myself up into the cab.

Abbi was there, Lula was there, both of them warm and alive against my frozen body, reaching across me to shut the door.

"Go," I said to Lula, my teeth chattering. "Drive!"

She put the truck in gear and hit the gas.

She cranked on the wheel, aiming us away from the house and back down the long gravel road.

I couldn't even see the road, had no idea how she could, other than she was not quite human. Her eyes were far better than mine.

A flash of taillights swam into view ahead of us. The hunters, leading us to a place to hide.

If we made it through this unholy storm.

Abbi hugged Lorde in a bear grip and whispered to Hado tucked into the crook of her other arm.

Hado's eyes flashed red, then he stretched and liqui-fied, becoming nothing but black smoke, a shadow that seeped through the wall of the cab, and back to the book hidden in the witch's box.

I didn't know if Hado could hide it from whatever was riding wild in the storm, but we needed every bit of help we could get to keep the book hidden.

"You're bleeding," Lu said, maybe had said more than once. She hadn't looked away from the road, away from the taillights fading in and out of sight, jostling and jerking in the gusting wind.

I didn't know how Pamela was keeping her vehicle on the road, or if she could see where she was going, but they'd said to follow them and there was no way in hell Lu was going to break that promise.

The storm was all around us now, the rain so loud on the roof, I couldn't hear the engine revving, couldn't hear Lorde, who was barking, her teeth bared.

She knew there were monsters in that storm—

—*power*—

—she knew something very bad was out there.

Lightning hissed, striking the ground beside us and exploding, the blast of thunder unbearable. I threw myself in front of Abbi, and reached for Lula, trying to keep them both safe from a threat I couldn't even name.

Was this Apep? Was the storm sent by Mithra? By Atë?

Or was there something else, something made of pure violence gunning for us?

Abbi screamed and pointed.

Lu slammed on the brakes.

The truck fish-tailed, rocking up on two wheels. I relived the crash we'd been in weeks ago, a crash I wasn't sure we would survive.

But Lu wrestled the wheel and held the truck to the road through sheer will alone.

The hunters had stopped ahead of us.

Not because of the rain.

But because there was a man standing there. No, not a man, a god.

He wore plain clothing, but his blond hair shone. As did the massive hammer in his hand.

The wind whipped around him, but he was a monolith, a mountain, a force against the storm that did not dare touch him.

"Is that?" Lula asked.

"I don't think…" I said.

"Thor," Abbi nodded. "The god of thunder."

"The storm. He's sent the storm to kill us," I said.

Abbi shook her head. "He's the god of protection too. And he's good. I know him. He's here to protect us." She pushed against my arm, straining forward. "Thor!" she yelled. "It's me! Moon Rabbit."

"Don't!" I said.

But it was too late. He lowered his head. The storm was rage, torment, impossible to penetrate. But he looked at her. Straight at her.

"Oh, shit." Lula put the truck into reverse, twisting to look over her shoulder.

"Go," I said. "Go."

Thor took a step. The sky roared with thunder. Another step. The next explosion nearly blew my ear drums. I ducked my head to my shoulder. Abbi screamed and covered both of her ears.

The god took another step, as unrelenting as the storm. His stride was supernaturally long, a pace no man could achieve. Fast, and growing faster.

"Thor?" Abbi said confused.

"Fuck," I breathed. "Drive, Lula, drive!"

But even with the truck at full throttle, we weren't gaining ground.

The god didn't pause, didn't slow. He grew larger, huge, his head lost in the churning sky, his power breaking the physics of this reality.

He was going to crash into us, step on us, smash us flat.

But moments before he was on us, moments before I knew he was going to run right into our truck or *through* it, he pulled back his arm.

His hand disappeared in the distance, and then whipped forward, his hammer flying straight at us.

CHAPTER EIGHT

I yelled and tightened my grip on Lula and Abbi, Lorde pinned between us all, bracing for the hammer's blow.

Time slowed. I wondered if Lula had thumbed the stem on the magic, time-stopping watch she wore.

But she couldn't have. Even with her inhumanly fast reflexes, there wasn't enough time for her to do anything more than reach for me.

The hammer struck the hood of the truck.

The truck and the whole dang world rang like a bell.

Sunlight blinded me.

Blue sky filled our windshield.

The storm was gone, as if it had never been there.

The truck was still, the engine dead.

We were in the middle of the road, not far from Eunice's house. The hunter's SUV several blocks ahead of us.

"What the hell was that?" I yelled.

Abbi squirmed against my grip. I leaned back into

the seat, dropping my arm. But not before squeezing Lula's once. She swallowed and nodded, acknowledging me.

She didn't look away from the window, her eyes wide with adrenalin.

"Thor," Abbi shoved at my arm again, and I moved it fully away from her. "He took the storm away. See? There's no storm. He did this." She waved her hands a little erratically at the world around us. "I told you. I told you he was good."

"He hit us with a hammer," I said. "Fuck. Just…" I mopped my shaking hand across my face, "…fuck."

"He hammered the storm away, Brogan," Abbi said, like I hadn't heard her the first time. "Not us, the storm."

"God storm," Lula said. "That was not natural. If he didn't call it up, who did?"

"I don't want to find out," I said. "Not while we're sitting still."

She swallowed. Her hand shook, but she started the truck. Silver's engine (thankfully) kicked over on the first try and we rolled up next to the hunters.

"Well holy hickory hell, Gauges," Pamela said when I rolled down my window. "How many gods hate you?"

"Too many. You still on for this? No hard feelings if you want to tap out now."

"Don't even think we'd leave you stranded. Family helps family. Stick tight and keep a weather eye. I'll get us there."

Elmer stuck his hand out the window and slapped the top of the car. "Let's go."

Pamela eased back onto the road and Lula's hand found mine. "There are wipes in the glove compartment," she said.

"For?"

"Your head. You're bleeding." I forgotten she'd said something about it after I'd been knocked on my ass. But now that she mentioned it, the headache growing behind my eyes made sense.

I fumbled with the glove compartment and pulled out the package of damp wipes. I dabbed one at my forehead, and Abbi shifted on her knees.

"Here. You're missing it." She took the wipe and scrubbed it firmly from my jaw to my temple.

I grunted at the pressure, but she didn't let up. "Turn your head so I can see where the cut is."

I did as she ordered. She poked at my hair, then hit a spot that sent stars across my vision and electricity down my spine.

I jerked and cupped my hand over the wound. "You don't have to stick your finger through my head."

"I need to clean it. Right Lula? I need to clean the cut."

"Brogan, let her clean it."

"For the love of…" I leaned back toward her and dropped my hand. "It's just a scrape."

Abbi was a little gentler when she parted my hair and dabbed at the wound, but it still smarted.

"Maybe stitches?" she said. "I…I don't know doctor stuff. I can heal it though, but I need my mortar and pestle and Hado and magic. Can I do magic?"

"No," Lula and I said at the same time.

"When we get to the hunter's place," Lula said. "You can use magic. Maybe. For now, a clean cloth or some napkins and put pressure on the wound."

"I can do it," I said.

"Me." Abbi smacked my hands away from the glove compartment. "I want to help."

The helplessness she felt was clear in her tone. She knew just how vulnerable we were out here where every god in existence seemed intent on tearing us off the face of the Earth.

I patted the edge of the seat, telling Lorde to hop down onto the floorboards. She jumped down and turned a circle, right in front of the glove compartment.

"Wait, no," Abbi said. "Lorde, your big fuzzy every-thing is in the way!"

Lorde *woof*ed at her and panted happily.

"Move, move," Abbi said, trying not to laugh.

I patted the seat again and Lorde jumped up and draped herself across my lap. "Who's a good girl?" I said, scratching behind her ears.

"Too much tail!" Abbi sputtered as Lorde wagged it right in her face. "Lorde!"

"You're the good girl," I said.

"Brogan! Now I can't reach your cut."

"Sure, you can." I turned my head. "Stretch."

Abbi made an exasperated sound but draped herself over Lorde and pressed the cloth on my head.

The cab of the truck wasn't really made for more than two, and with a large fluffy dog, a large man (me), Lula, and Abbi all shoved into it, it was downright crowded.

Still, Abbi made it work, laughing as Lorde pretzeled back to lick her face. "You're making it hard on purpose," Abbi grumped.

"Just a little. I can hold it now. How about you give Lorde a pet. She's worried."

Abbi dropped back into her seat. She was still frowning, but some of the fear, some of the panic had eased out of her. I could tell by the softening of her hands, the looseness in her shoulders, the narrowed eyes which held no real anger.

"Lorde likes me more anyway, don't you, Lordey?" she said.

Lorde, the traitor, barked happily, and scrabbled to turn in the small space so she could flop on her back, her head almost in Lula's lap.

Abbi scrubbed her fuzzy belly and chest and cooed at her.

I glanced over at Lula, and her smile, even though it was tight, told me she knew what I was doing. Knew I was trying to keep Abbi, keep Lula, hell, keep myself calm.

With Abbi fully occupied petting and laughing at Lorde, I did what Pamela had asked and kept an eye skyward.

I didn't expect every god, or even every threat to come from the sky. But on this long stretch of the Route spooling out before us, it was more sky than earth—sky for years.

Lula sent us hurtling through that sky, following the hunters. We had hours to drive, and daylight to burn.

I just hoped Hado, wrapped around the book, could

keep the power and magic of the thing hidden long enough for us to get wherever we were getting without attracting another god.

The miles and hours rolled out, one after the other. The sky remained blue, the car ahead of us kept a steady pace, and by all appearance, it was a beautiful late-summer day.

After a bit, we pulled off for a roadside meal provided by the bags Eunice had sent with us, refueled, and made it to New Mexico in good time.

When the hunters slowed to turn onto a dirt road which was nothing more than two overgrown ruts, the sun had settled in the west, not behind the horizon yet, but heavy and liquid, burning gold.

We rattled down the track for over an hour. Even with the windows up, dust filled the cab, covering the dash, the windows, and us.

We had a quarter tank of gas and two five-gallon cans in the back. It would be enough to get us back to the road, but I didn't know if it would be enough to get us to the closest gas station.

"How much farther?" I asked, even though neither Lula or Abbi would know.

"There!" Abbi pointed at some random spot in the distance. "We're going there."

Lula squinted. "I don't see anything."

"I can…" Abbi said. "It's…I can tell. I think it's pretty old. Well, not old like me, but old."

"What do you see?" Lu asked.

"They're turning to it. See?"

All I saw were piles of rocks, which was all there was

to see out here except for the occasional jack rabbit, lizard, or red-tailed hawk.

"No," I said.

"Look better," Abbi said, frustrated.

Lu slowed the truck, giving the dust Pamela's car was kicking up extra time to settle. Pamela drove between piles of rocks.

That's when I could actually see it.

The tunnel was so cleverly hidden with natural camouflage and magic that I would have driven—hell, I would have walked—right past it and not known it was there.

It was just wide and tall enough for a car. Pamela drove into it. After a moment, we did too.

Daylight cut off faster than I'd expected and I blinked, waiting for my eyes to adjust. The magic made it seem like there was only so far a person could wander into the place before the tunnel dead ended.

The darkness felt complete, unbroken for several minutes. Then it shimmered, and lights positioned alongside the road appeared. They were just bright enough, I could see the tunnel was not natural, but man made.

"Military?" I suggested.

Lula nodded. "Lots of old silos and other things out here."

"It's the other things I don't like." Abbi reached for my hand and held on tight.

Just a few weeks ago, we'd all descended into the caverns in Missouri to fight the Hush. We'd saved Hado, who had been stolen from Abbi and tortured.

But it was Abbi, well, Abbi and Hado on their own, with nothing but her mortar and pestle and moon powers that had sealed those caves.

The Hush would be trapped there, in the darkness for years to come.

I still had nightmares of those caves, those monsters, that fight. Abbi had faced more than me. I knew from the sounds she made in her sleep that she had nightmares too.

She blinked hard, tears pooled in her eyes, but she didn't look away from the darkness around us.

"Elmer, Pamela, and Josie are good people," I said. "They fought the Hush with us. They wanted to look after you, remember?"

"I know. It's just…dark and cave-y in here."

"Bah. What's a little darkness? We have a moon rabbit who can shine almost as bright as the sun."

Her scowl was fierce. "Brighter than the sun. I killed vampires. All of them."

"Damn right you did."

Brake lights bathed the space in red, and Lula slowed the truck. Then the SUV rolled to the right and we followed.

Darkness fell away like a magician's cape.

We were in a brightly lit garage where three other cars were stored. More lights snapped on automatically as the SUV took one of the dozen open parking spaces.

Lu maneuvered into the space next to them.

I whistled. "This is nice."

And it was.

White subway tiles accented in dark green, gave the

garage the distinctive Art Deco style that used to be more common back in my day. Accents of dark wood gave another hint at the care taken in building this place.

Pamela and the others got out of the car, and so did we, though I was stiff and groaned a bit.

"Everyone still in one piece?" Elmer asked.

"Never better," I said, trying to ignore the headache.

"Was this military?" Lula asked.

"Intelligence services," Josie said. "Lots of spy stuff happened here."

"For the world wars?" I asked.

"To begin with," Elmer said. "After that, it was decommissioned. The last keyholder passed those keys on to some local monster hunters. Ever since..." He made his way across the space and up a short set of metal stairs. "Ever since, it's been in the family. The hunting family."

He used a key to unlock the door and slapped the inside of the wall. Lights came alive in the room ahead of him. "Come on in," he said. "Family's always welcome."

"We're part of the hunting family, right?" Abbi asked me.

"Dunno, Pumpkin. Ask Pamela."

"Of course you are." Pamela draped the strap of a duffle over one shoulder and hefted two others out of the back of the car. "Family are the only people allowed. Come on this way. I'll show you your rooms."

Josie shut the car doors. "You're gonna love the

showers. Hot water for days. Nice watch, by the way," she said to Lu. "Antique?"

The magic pocket watch that could stop time, and the winged key to open the book, hung from separate chains around Lu's neck. She usually kept them hidden, but our run through the storm had dislodged them so they were on the outside of her shirt.

"Yes," Lu said smoothly, tucking it away. "It's very old."

"Well, old fits in here." Josie strode across the room. "You won't believe how far back the library goes."

Abbi took a step, then turned back.

"Maybe I'll stay out here in the truck."

"Why?" Lu asked. She had grabbed our bags and handed me mine.

Abbi rocked up on tiptoes and pointed at the tool box. "Hado will miss me."

Lu frowned.

I leaned on the truck. "Let's find out what kind of magic they have on this place. See how safe it would be for Hado to move away from the book. If it's not good enough or safe enough, we'll all sleep out here with Hado together."

"A sleepover?" Abbi asked.

"Yup. A sleepover."

Lu's gaze darted up to mine, and she smiled.

"We might be part of the hunters' family now," I said, "but we're our own little family first."

"Yay!" Abbi said. "But I'm going to stay here with Hado."

Lorde woofed and put her paws on the bumper.

Lu scrubbed Lorde's ears. "You stay here and look after Abbi, okay, girl?"

Lorde wagged her tail.

"In you go." Lu pulled down the tailgate, and Abbi and Lorde jumped in.

"I'll put out all the blankets just in case!" Abbi opened the storage bins and dragged out the quilts, sleeping bags, and pillows, shaking them with wild abandon while Lorde barked and nipped.

"That leaves me and you to see if the living situation works." I took a step.

Lu put her hand on my arm and tugged.

"What…?"

She stepped around and into me, her body pressing against mine, as if I were shelter from a storm and she was freezing.

I wrapped my arms around her. "Hey now," I said. "What's this? Are you okay?"

She nodded, then pulled back, her hands on either side of my face.

"I'm fine. How badly are you hurt? Tell me the truth. I thought the storm was going to tear you to pieces."

"I have a headache," I said, "but vision and hearing are good. It was a knock on the head, not a concussion. I might have bruised my ass when I fell, but I'm fine, Lula. I'm still on my feet. Still standing."

"I won't lose you, Brogan Gauge. I won't." She moved just that much more into me and drew my head down.

Then she kissed me, harder than I'd expected, urgent, needful.

I met her intensity, then slowly gentled my embrace, running my palm down her back and up again, threading my fingers in her silky hair.

I gentled my mouth too, easing the kiss, soothing her with slower, softer touches, my breath even and calm.

She relaxed by inches, but did not take her hands off my face, holding me just where she wanted me, keeping me, claiming me.

I tasted salt as her tears caught between our lips.

Finally, finally she pulled back, her gaze searching my face, making sure I was still there, still holding her.

"As if I would ever leave your side. Not even death can keep me from you."

"I know," she whispered, "I know." She released my face and rested her head against my shoulder.

"I love you," I said.

"I love you," she said.

"I love pie!" Abbi announced, and I could feel Lula's smile.

"We'll find you a carrot," I offered.

"Yay! I like carrots!"

Lorde barked.

"And a bone for Lorde." Abbi wrapped her arms around the dog's neck and pulled her down beside her, making Lorde squirm and wag her tail.

"Sounds like we have our orders," I said.

Lu leaned back. "She's not the boss of us. We don't have to listen."

"I can hear you!" Abbi said.

Lu moved to the stairs, her body language shifting into high alert.

"You think we're in danger?"

She shook her head. "Still. I walk into the room first."

There was a reason she took point in unknown situations. Even though I was a big man and a strong man, she was *thrawn*. Being half-vampire meant she was stronger than me, faster than me, and could heal a lot quicker than I could.

It didn't make her invulnerable, but with her reflexes, she could respond to an attack before I even knew what hit us.

The hallway at the top of the stairs was well lit, built of dark wood with a deep green-and-gold wallpaper. Fixtures in the ceiling gave off a warm light, and the hall branched in two directions.

"This way," Pamela said from where she was waiting for us on the left. "Figured you'd want to pick out beds first. Where's Abbi?"

"Truck," Lula said. "We need to know what kind of magical and practical protections you have in this place."

"Sure thing. We'll head to the control room instead."

She crossed to the right hall, and after a few turns (I was mentally mapping how the hall worked as a defensive structure), it spilled us out into a beautiful room.

I whistled again. "This is very nice."

More of the dark wood accented the space, with dark green subway tiles at the bottom half of the walls, wallpaper on the top, and wood inlaid floors.

The walls were high enough to cover two stories, but instead of an upper floor, exposed brass staircases led to a loft which lined the entire well-lit upper space.

Bookshelves racked back from the open loft rooms and a handful of padded chairs littered the area.

But the main room, the control room, was set much like I would expect a military space to be arranged. There were maps on one wall (marked with push pins), and a mix of wooden and metal storage cabinets, with doors and drawers, set at strategic positions.

Centering the room was a large wooden table that could seat twelve, matching chairs drawn up tight.

The table held a variety of crystals, small tokens, silk bags, and other magical bits and twigs on one side, looking as if they'd been dropped there after a treasure hunt. A few leather-bound books were stacked at the far end.

"Don't mind the mess," Pamela said. "We left in a hurry last time we were here."

"I'll get these out of the way." Josie scooped up the books. "Be right back."

She took the nearest staircase to the upper level.

"Kitchen's that way," Elmer pointed at the door on one end of the room. "Bedrooms back that way. Main library there," then to another door to a room set at what I thought was west, "and various other rooms that way, including a safe room. So. Think this will do for you?"

"What magical defenses do you have?" Lula asked. "How hidden is this place, really?"

"You won't find anywhere with more magical wards

or spells," Pamela said. "Nothing can find us here. No gods, monsters, or humans can cross our trip lines without us knowing it."

"How do you know someone's crossed the trip lines?" Lu asked.

A mechanical snap cracked the air, and every light dimmed. Red emergency lights flooded the place.

An alarm wailed.

The line had been tripped.

The hunters pulled weapons.

Josie, from above said, "Entrance."

Lu drew her knives.

"Abbi," I said. I pivoted and ran back to the garage, Lu on my heels.

Abbi stood in the back of the truck, her magic mortar and pestle in her hands, Lorde on guard next to her.

"Are you okay?" I asked, reaching over the side of the truck to touch her arm.

"Someone's out there," she said.

"Good evening, Gauges," a male voice echoed through the garage, the halls, the rooms. "We need to talk."

CHAPTER NINE

The alarm silenced, but everything was still bathed in red light.

"*Who?*" Lula mouthed.

Abbi tipped her head to the side, a motion so like a rabbit it would have been cute if the secret bolt hole—that no monster, god, or man could find—hadn't just been found.

"Ricky?" Abbi asked.

I shook my head. Ricky was Lula's, well, now also my, good friend. She was a Crossroads, a person who guarded a magical house near Route 66 where all manners of supernaturals could claim sanctuary.

But that was a male voice, not Ricky's.

"I know you're not alone," the voice said. "I promise you, I am here to help you."

I rolled my eyes. We'd heard that so many times, it was ridiculous.

"Wizard." Pamela strode into the garage, a scrying crystal glowing in her hand. "Here, I'll show you."

She sprinkled what looked like sand over the crystal.

The glow caught the sand, growing flat and bright over the bowl until it was the size of a small movie screen.

A bird's eye view appeared in the glow, angled from above looking down. It swooped then hovered in front of a man.

He was built strong, like a rugby player, his bare arms tattooed with overlapping designs which flowed and shifted across his skin. He wore a brown shirt, tan pants, and had a twig of a pecan tree tucked behind his ear.

His intensely green eyes were narrowed and every inch of him signaled high alert.

"Cardamom," Lu said.

Even though the crystal's view was a little foggy, she was right. It was Ricky's half-dryad wizard boyfriend.

At least it appeared to be him. There was no reason for him to be in New Mexico, much less in the middle of nowhere.

"You know him?" Pamela asked.

"Ricky's boyfriend," Lu said.

"Ricky Vargas?"

"Yes."

"Haven't met him."

"He recently came back into her life," Lu said.

"But he's a wizard, right?"

"Half-dryad wizard."

"Huh. Well, I'm not inclined to believe he showed up here minutes after we did by accident," Pamela said.

"Don't let him in," I said. "It might be an illusion."

"Not even my tenth rodeo, Brogan. We have ways to see what he really is. Hold tight."

She jogged back into the building, taking the crystal with her.

I wanted to follow her but didn't want to leave Abbi and the book alone.

"You folks worried about leaving the book out here?" Elmer asked as he came down the stairs like he was a man in his fifties, not his eighties.

"Yes," Lu said.

"I'm not thrilled about it either. How about we use this to take it to the safe room?" He pulled a black cloth out of his pocket and flapped it in the air. "This whole place is a vault, but that safe room doesn't even register as a blip on this Earth."

"Shadow cloth!" Abbi said. "I like those. Here, let me."

Elmer gave her the cloth. She opened the tool box and retrieved the witch's box with the book hidden inside.

She wrapped the cloth around the box, and the hissing I'd been hearing for days stopped.

I stuck a finger in my ear and jiggled it. "You hear that?" I asked Lu.

"No?"

"Neither do I." I hadn't realized the book had been making noise—the slightest whispering, like water over stones, or the shift of sand under foot. It had been so subtle, I hadn't realized how constant it was.

"It makes a sound," I said. "It's quiet now."

"That cloth smothers any magic it touches," Elmer

said. "Got it off an old witch who'd once hunted the Strange."

Abbi clambered out of the truck, the box in her arms. "Maybe we should do it fast."

"Let's go then." Elmer jogged up the stairs, Abbi on his heels.

Lorde jumped out of the truck and came over to Lula and me, asking for head scratches. She wasn't frightened or on guard anymore, which was a good sign for a dog who had been around a lot of magic and knew what danger looked like.

She bounded after Abbi.

"Thoughts on the place? On Cardamom?" I asked Lu, as we climbed the stairs again.

"They haven't let him in yet," she said. "They're cautious, which is good. You can really hear it? The book?"

"I could. It's a hiss, or a whisper. Like static. But it's silent under the shadow cloth."

"So, they have strong magical items and the knowledge of how to use them. I like that, too."

"Are we staying?"

"Maybe."

"Maybe," I agreed. Could we trust that their magic would hold strong against everyone and everything tracking us? I doubted it. But if it could buy us enough time to find a weapon that would kill Headwaters, it was worth the risk.

"Hey," Josie waved us into a side alcove just off the control room. "Pamela's checking on our visitor. We can watch from here."

This room had screens—some of them computer, some of them older gear that looked like radar, and other technology I wasn't familiar with.

An array of crystals sat in a circle on a small lit table in the center of the room, crystals that looked like the one Pamela had used earlier.

Josie did the sand trick over the table of crystals and they responded, showing a sky view that lowered to eye level.

Cardamom stood in the same place as before, sweating in the heat, but otherwise he looked calm.

The perspective shifted, and we got a view of the side of him, the back of him, the side, and front again.

I didn't see Pamela in any of those angles, but I had a feeling she was the one controlling the view.

"We have tests that will tell us if he's who he says he is," Josie said. "Make sure he's not under any contracts, trapped by a *geas*, or working for someone who wants to harm you or us."

"What kind of tests?" Lula asked.

"Pam's doing them now. It's a mix of things. Magic, of course. Some physical test equipment that can give bio readings from a distance. And our secret weapon, the sniffer."

"Okay, I'll bite," I said. "What's a sniffer?"

"That." Josie pointed at the image.

A very small lizard, about the length of my thumb skittered out from under a rock. It was no different than every other lizard out there that bobbed up to the warm tops of rocks or dipped back down in the shadows.

It didn't approach Cardamom or do anything strange.

It was (to be generous) the plainest looking dirt-brown lizard I'd ever seen.

Cardamon didn't appear to notice it either.

"Is it magic?"

"Not really, but yes, a little. We found it, oh, I don't know, twenty years ago? It'd been living in the archives, hibernating. It just popped up and wanted the banana Elmer was eating. You should have seen that fight. Hilarious. We didn't understand its ability until we ran into some ghouls. The little guy really came in handy."

"A lizard," Lula said. "It can smell magic?"

"Yes, but more importantly it can sense the intent and threat of a person or thing."

"We're trusting a lizard?" I crossed my arms. "That's not weird at all."

"Is that any weirder than being an earthbound spirit, who may or may not be able to wield the spell book of the gods, and who is traveling with the actual rabbit from the actual moon?"

Lu covered her mouth and snorted.

"But a lizard," I said.

"Oh, it's not just a lizard," Elmer said coming into the space with glasses of water for us all. "It's dragon kind."

"Dragon?" Abbi pushed forward to better see what was, admittedly, a pretty boring scene of a man standing in the desert.

"Dragon *kind*. Not a full dragon, but...dragon adjacent," Elmer said.

"Like a dragon pet? A dog or cat, but dragon?" Abbi asked.

Elmer held his finger and thumb slightly apart. "More like a tiny little dragon wizard."

"Oh," Abbi breathed. "Why does it look like a lizard?"

"Because that's what it wants to look like," Josie said.

Abbi nodded. "It's okay to look like what you want to look like."

She should know, since I was pretty sure her true form was actually a rabbit.

The lizard ducked down into the shadow and for the barest second, even though I had eyes on it, it disappeared. Then it reappeared and darted out from under the rock.

"Clear," Josie said.

"How do you know?" Lu asked.

She tapped her forehead. "It said so."

I just blinked, letting that sink in.

Elmer handed Lu a glass of water. "I know we're asking you to put your trust in us, but Eunice agreed this was the place where you'd be safe. So did Bo and Raven. If you trust them, you can trust us. And we trust the lizard."

"I *super* trust the lizard," Abbi said.

"I have a better idea," I said. "How about we call Ricky? See if she knows if Cardamom was headed this way."

Lu huffed, annoyed she hadn't thought about that. "Do you have cell service?"

"Clear as a bell," Elmer said.

I took a glass of water and downed half in one go. It was sweet and refreshingly cold.

Lu took her phone out of her pocket and called.

"Ricky, hi," she said. "Do you know where Cardamom is right now?"

I could hear Ricky's voice even though Lula held the phone to her ear.

"Hello to you too. Are you okay? The house was really worried about all of you."

"Thank the house. We're fine at the moment. Is Cardamom with you?"

"No. He left to find you. Did he?"

"Someone's here who looks like him," Lu said.

"Oh, we're being *that* level of suspicious. Okay. Can you see his left hand?"

We all looked back at the display.

"Yes."

"There's a tattoo he only ever shows when he's proving who he is. In other words, nothing which can duplicate, clone, mask, or appear as someone else can ever get that tattoo right."

"What is it?" I asked.

"What is it?" Lula repeated.

"It's a circle at the base of his thumb. In the center is a star. A silver star. As you look at it, it will rotate counter-clockwise between silver, gold, and green."

His hands were clasped in front of him, left over right so we could see the circle and the star.

"Do you see it?" Ricky asked.

"Yes," Lula said.

"Then that's Cardamom. We know what you're

trying to do," she said, wisely not announcing the book or us wanting to kill Headwaters. "He thinks he can help."

"Why aren't *you* here?" I asked a little louder.

"Because I'll be more help here. Call me if you need anything. The house is looking for items or information that will give you guidance with the object you're dealing with."

"Thank you," Lu said.

"You can do this," Ricky said. "I know you can."

Lu thumbed off the call. "It's him. It's Cardamom."

"I'll let Pamela know to bring him in," Josie said. "She'll lead him through the west door. That will dump them into a containment room. They'll stay there for at least fifteen minutes. Overabundance of caution, but now's not the time to skimp."

"Oh, we agree," Lu said.

"You have time if you want to pick out a room," Elmer said. "They won't be inside for at least a half hour. That is, if you've decided to stay with us."

"We have," I said.

There might be a safer place along the Route to find a magical weapon or to try using the spell book of the gods, but I didn't know where it would be.

Besides, the Walches were family and had adopted us as such. They were not only offering every resource they had—physical and magical—to us, they were doing it at great risk to themselves.

"Down the hall," Elmer said. "You know the way. My room's first on the left. The girls have the first on the right. Any other is open for the taking."

We walked into the control room where we'd dumped our duffels and bags, and then to the bedroom wing of the place.

Abbi skipped ahead of us, opening every door and making *ooh* and *ahh* noises as she looked into the rooms. The last door on the right made her stop. Then she ran to it. "I want this one!"

Each room was pretty much the same on either side. They held two twins or a double bed, wood floors with rugs beneath the beds. The walls were wood and brick and there were shelves and bedside tables or dressers.

The bedding was clean, functional, and in no way new. The pillows were plump enough I knew they were good quality feather.

"You picked the one the farthest from the kitchen?" I asked Abbi. "Are you sure?"

I looked in the room. Abbi was sprawled on the bed, arms akimbo. Hado, who apparently was done guarding the book, curled on her chest in kitten form, purring.

"Oh," Lula said. "Look at that."

Everything about the room was identical to the others except the ceiling.

The ceiling was painted midnight blue with a huge, accurate full moon in an arc of constellations and planets, each carefully identified in clean gold writing.

"I like this one," Abbi sighed. "The moon is the best."

"We'll take the one across the hall," Lula said.

"That puts us farthest from the kitchen, too, you know," I said.

Lu patted my arm. "The least of our problems."

She turned the light on and walked into our room.

I unloaded the duffle onto the dresser.

"Two twin beds," I said. "You telling me something, Lula Gauge?"

She threw me a look, then shoved one bed over to the other. "You think I want to sleep alone after all these years?"

"I tend to snore."

"So do I."

"Well, I don't mind," I said. "Never have."

She drew her hand back through her hair, then rubbed her forehead. "Today's been a lot."

"Too damn many gods," I said. "I mean, Thor? Really?"

That got a smile out of her.

"Want some rest?" I asked.

"No." She sat and patted the bed. "Sit with me a minute though?"

"As long as you want." The bed springs made some noise as I lowered myself beside her, but they were stiff and strong. I put my arm behind her back, pulling her into me.

She tucked her head into my shoulder, just like she had out in the garage. The events of the last day, hell, the last months and longer…the events of our entire damned lives…seemed to pile up all at once.

It was exhausting.

"How the hell are we going to figure out how to use the book, Brogan?" she asked. "God power? You and me?"

I hummed and stroked my thumb across the back of her hand resting on my knee.

"What if we just don't?"

"That's not an option. We're killing Headwaters."

"Even Raven said there might be other weapons that can kill Headwaters."

Her eyes, when she tipped her face up, glowed gold. "How long would it take us to find another weapon—if there even is one close to the Route? How much time do we have before the gods hunting us find us? And out there?" She waved at the wall. "They will find us in an instant."

"We aren't wizards, Lu. We don't wield magic. Do you really think we can just pick up the spell book of the *gods* and use it? No. It's smarter—and a hell of a lot safer—to find some other damned weapon."

"Is there one? We don't know. Two gods couldn't tell us if there was another weapon that would kill Headwaters without killing us. Remember? Killing Headwaters means we die too."

She shook her head. "We have the book. The lost god spells are our only chance of surviving this. We use the weapon at hand."

"How?" I asked, frustrated. "Even the gods don't know how to use it. Just because our souls were torn apart and stitched back together to make us into tools to use the book, doesn't mean we know how. There are no instructions for the damn thing."

"Ricky said she'd look for instructions."

"She's not going to find anything. Even the gods forgot that book existed."

Lu shifted in my embrace, drawing closer, sensing my racing heartbeat, my instinctive panic over the very idea of using the book. That book had already been the reason I had been killed, and Lu turned into a *thrawn*.

I hated everything about it.

"We'll take it slow," she said. "Small steps. Small spells, if that's possible. Trial and error. We can do it. We've figured out hard things before."

"We don't have time for that."

"We do. We'll take as long as we damned well want. This hideout is so far off grid, I don't think even Atë or Mithra can find it."

"Cardamon found it," I said.

"Let's ask him how. I bet Eunice or Raven told him."

I grunted. I hadn't thought about that obvious possibility.

"This place looks like it can survive an apocalypse," she went on. "Elmer said they have a safe room where no magic can escape. We can work with the book there."

"Or we could just grab the book and run to Ordinary. Forget about killing Headwaters."

One red eyebrow rose, and she held my gaze. "We're killing Headwaters." Her words were soft but as inescapable and heavy as a coffin's lid.

I looked away and tried to steady my breathing. There was no arguing or reasoning her out of this decision. This was the one thing she'd been living for all these years. She wouldn't give it up now it was within her grasp.

"If it's too hard to use the spells," I said, "if it's too dangerous…"

"*Then* we kill Headwaters no matter the consequences. And take Atë down. There will be *no* god who will tell us if we deserve to live our lives or not. *Our* lives, Brogan. Together. Nothing will take you away from me again."

"Damn right," I growled. "Fuck those gods."

She nodded and exhaled, the circles beneath her eyes like bruises in this light.

I gently touched her cheek and was surprised at the heat of her skin. "You sure you don't want a couple minutes of rest before we deal with the wizard?"

"Yes. I'm also sure I want you to kiss me."

That was a request I would never refuse.

CHAPTER TEN

The wizard was sipping tea. "It was the star tattoo, right?" Cardamom asked.

We had gathered at the long wooden table in the control room.

Cardamom looked relaxed and tan, his sandy hair sun-streaked, as if he'd spent the entire summer out in the orchards. Since he was half-dryad, I could only assume he had.

"Ricky told us," Lula said.

"I hoped you'd call her."

"Why didn't you just tell us who you were?" I asked.

"Because I wasn't a hundred percent sure you were here. If I'd gotten the place wrong, I didn't want it leading back to Ricky."

"How did you find it?" Elmer asked. "Because if we have a leak, I'm gonna need to plug that hole."

That wouldn't sound as threatening if he didn't have his rifle in pieces on the table and was slowly notching it back together after he'd thoroughly cleaned it.

"Euterpe told me. She said you'd be here."

"Did she show up in a dream?" I asked, remembering my own first encounter with the Muse.

"No, she pulled up at Ricky's about a week ago and asked to have a chat. The house was so excited a Muse was visiting, it conjured up all the fancy china and furniture and put out the best tea and cookies it could get its magical hands on."

"A week ago," Lula said. "She must think we're predictable."

Cardamom shrugged. "She gave me seven different possibilities. This was number two."

"You want to tell us the others?" I asked.

"I can. But now we're here, all the other possible futures have been altered."

"Free will," Lu said.

"That's it," he agreed.

"Did she tell you why you were supposed to be here?" Pamela asked.

"Little bit of free will in that too," he said. "So, no. Just that I might want to lend my services. I do know Lula and Brogan have the spell book of the gods."

"That's right," Lula said. "What does that have to do with you?"

"I can only guess it's because I'm a wizard. I have extensive training with magical tomes and ancient spells."

"You rank high in the guild?" Elmer asked.

Cardamom's eyes seemed to darken, but his voice was still steady, friendly. "High enough."

That made Elmer grunt.

I could tell Cardamom was underplaying his ability. I wondered if it was out of habit, or if he had a reason to hide.

"You can't touch it," I said. "The book. No one can."

"How did you transport it?"

"Witch's box," Lula said.

"Someone picked it up, put it in the box?"

Lu nodded.

"Look." He leaned back, easy like there was nothing on the line with this decision. "I'm good at this stuff. You're Ricky's best friends. If you're going to be dumb enough to try and use god magic, the least I can do is try to help you stay alive, point out possible traps, help decipher language.

"You can say no," he said amiably, "and I'll get out of your hair. But if you want my knowledge and skill, I'm here for you."

"They teach you how to wield god power in this wizard school you graduated from?" Pamela asked.

"No. But they teach us how to wield power. Any power."

There was something about how he said it that sent warning chills down my spine.

"You haven't asked us what we want to use the book for," Lula said.

"It's not like I'm not curious, and knowing what kind of spells you want to use would help me guide you. But Ricky loves you. That means I've got your back, because I know you have hers."

"I think you should say yes," Abbi said. She was on

the floor pulling a string with a knotted end for Hado to chase.

"Let's just get to the point," Josie said. "What's the downside of having a wizard help with the magic?"

I rubbed my face. "Death, I suppose. Messing with the book could kill us, but there's an even higher chance it would kill you, Card. Then what would Ricky think?"

"She'd think I was a dumbass for not setting up protections." He gestured with his teacup, the tattoos on the backs of his hands glowing. "I, my friends, am not a dumbass."

"Maybe the lizard can help," Abbi said. "I liked the lizard."

"Lizard?" Cardamom asked.

Elmer cleared his throat. "Never mind that. Are you two going to do this or not?"

I didn't have to look at Lu to know what her answer would be.

This was big—trying to use god powers, god spells, trying to understand the book to find the lost gods' spells. Lu and I weren't trained for it.

We knew magic. We'd been around it all our lives.

But we were not wizards.

Was it a stroke of luck Cardamom had come back into Ricky's life just when we needed a wizard?

Yes.

Was I suspicious about that coincidence?

Also, yes.

But we were at the point of no return. We'd made our deals with gods, with monsters, with seers and demons. If we wanted justice—to kill the monster who had destroyed our lives—if we wanted to make sure neither Atë nor any other god could ever get their hands on the book again, then there were risks we had to take.

Cardamom was a risk I was willing to take.

"Let's get you in the same room as the book," I said. "Find out if it knocks you out or not."

"Fun," he said. "When do we start?"

Lula stood. "Now."

"Later," I said. "I don't remember when we last slept. I say we eat, get some rest, and hit it early in the morning."

We had ourselves a little glare off, my wife and I. Then she cut her gaze to the side. "How much time do you think we have before someone or something else finds this bolt hole?"

"I'd wager six hours, minimum," I said. "Enough time for food, and a couple hours sleep."

"Food will be ready in a bit," Pamela said. "I put on a roast and sides. There's cornbread in the oven. Eunice sent some extra food too."

"Sounds delicious." Cardamom stood and pushed his chair flush with the table. "Need any help? I'm handy in the kitchen."

Pamela sized him up from head to foot. "I think you're exactly the kitchen help I've been looking for. This way, Wizard."

He chuckled. "Just Card works."

"Oh, I'll make sure you work, Just Card."

They pushed through the swinging door into the kitchen, leaving me, Lula, Abbi, and Elmer in the room.

"I'm gonna take a walk," Elmer said. "Make sure

the trips and guards are solid. Tell the girls to save me some of that grub."

He picked up his rifle and cleaning kit then walked out of the room.

"I think Cardamom is going to be a big help." Abbi came over and took Lula's hand. "Even the lizard thinks so."

"You're talking to the lizard?" Lu asked.

Abbi shrugged one shoulder, her head tipped. "It kind of talks to me? It likes Card's magic. But…"

"But?" I asked when she didn't go on.

"It says lots and lots and lots of bad people are looking for him."

"Terrific," I said. "He's on the run too."

"That's okay," Abbi said. "We can run really fast."

A pot clattered in the kitchen and laughter rolled out. This wasn't my home. Hell, I hadn't had a home for as long as I could remember. Well, not a physical building.

Lula was my home. Had always been. So long as she was in my life, I was home. I belonged.

But it was nice to be here, in a place that offered shelter, maybe long enough we could take a breath.

I jerked my thumb toward the kitchen and the laughter. "Want to get in on that?" I asked Lula.

She stared at the door. I knew she missed baking and always spent time in Ricky's kitchen when she got the chance.

"No." She looked back at me, her gaze sharp. "I think that will keep them busy long enough you and I can see if the safe room is robust enough."

"After that we sleep?"

"Eat, then sleep. Yes." She stood. "Do you want to come, Abbi?"

Abbi looked over her shoulder, her nose wrinkled. Lorde was snoring on a pile of blankets Josie had set out for her. Hado was sneaking up to her, either to pounce attack, or snuggle in for a snooze.

Abbi nodded. "Hado can stay here."

Hado's little kitten ear twitched, the only indication he'd heard her.

I pushed up to my feet and stretched. I was bruised and sore, but still breathing, and that's what counted.

"That way, right?" I took a step, and my thigh cramped. I hissed and took the weight off of it, limping toward the hall.

"How bad?" Lu was beside me, moving with the kind of silence and speed only a half-vampire could. "You're limping."

"Just a cramp."

She walked alongside me, frowning.

"I'd tell you if it was worse."

She exhaled, wanting to say something, then changed her mind.

"Years ago, after Mithra tried to kill us," she said. "We promised each other we'd never deal with gods again."

"I remember."

"And now…"

"…and now we're up to our armpits in gods," I said. "I know. I don't see a way out of it. The only way forward is to get the book to Ordinary and hope they don't wipe us off the face of the Earth on the way."

"Headwaters dies first," she said.

"Agreed. Which means we can't run. Not yet."

"This one," Abbi said, stopping outside a nondescript door.

"The minute we get the chance," I said, "we tell every damn one of the gods to pound sand."

She flashed me a quick smile then blew out a breath, her stance settling into the wary preparedness of impending battle.

The safe room door could only be unlocked with the key Pamela had given Lu, and only if Lu used it. Lu had hooked the key onto a chain with the winged key to the spell book. A separate chain suspended the pocket watch that could stop time.

Lu bent and inserted the key into the keyhole. The door flushed with blue-white light, sigils catching fire and spreading to kindle more magical guards and symbols along the walls.

She pushed open the door.

I took a deep breath and forced myself to step into the room.

Stone floor and concrete walls, the space was big enough to walk around in and also to hold a cot and small side table set up along one wall. There were no windows.

The room was absolutely soaked in magic, smelling of pine, of all things, beneath a metallic tang of copper.

Electric lights from above burned yellow, and a fan

set high in the ceiling cut the light into slow wedges that rotated around the room.

The floor was carved, painted, chalked, and salted with more magical sigils, containments, and spells than you could shake a witch at.

Right there in the middle of the spells, in the middle of the floor, covered by the black shadow cloth, was the witch's box containing the book.

"I'll shut the door." Abbi darted back to make sure it closed.

The click was absolutely claustrophobic.

I rolled my shoulders and stuck my hand in my back pocket to keep from grabbing Lula and getting us both the hell out of here. "All right. How are we going to approach this?"

"Lula should touch it," Abbi said. "I mean, then we'll know if the room magic can hold the book magic in."

"How?" The enormity of the task ahead of us seemed impossible. I felt lost already. "How will we know if the gods can tell that we're touching it or using it?"

Abbi tipped her round face up, her nose wrinkled, her eyes sparkling with mischief. "I can see them, Brogan." She made her eyes go wide. "I have big ears too."

She leaned into my arm, then skipped to the far side of the room. "I'm looking. I promise. If I see a god, I can tell you and you can shove the book back in the witch's box. Easy!"

"Easy," I muttered.

"No instructions," Lula said. "We could wait for Cardamom, but we just need to see if the wards are strong enough to contain the magic."

"Can't test the wards with the book in the box," I said. "Unless…we could do this tomorrow."

"And spend the night worrying about it?" She wasn't calling me a coward, but yeah, she was calling me a coward.

"Hell." I moved toward the box.

Lu stopped with the toes of her boots outside the painted line that created a circle around the box. I stopped beside her.

"Think we need permission to step in the circle?" I asked.

"Abbi?" Lu asked.

"Elmer didn't ask for permission when I put the box there," she said. "He said we could cross in and out. But the book couldn't."

I mopped my hand over my face. I was sweating, even though the room was several degrees colder than the rest of the hideout. "On three?"

"Three." Lula stepped forward.

I stepped after her.

No explosions, no light show, no affect at all.

"Abbi?" I asked.

"Nothing. No gods."

Lula pulled the chain over her head and took the few steps to the box. "Do you want to pick up the box?"

"Yeah." If she was the only one who could touch the book, I should be the one who held the box.

I bent and removed the cloth.

The box was the size of a small cooler and looked like a wooden crate that might hold tools. The wood was unfinished, chipped on the edges, and all-in-all looked like it would fit right in at a thrift shop.

But the inside of the box was woven with the McClellan witches' power and magic—moonlight and forest, water and glade, all grown into the very fiber of the wood.

It was powerful enough to hide the book from gods, even when those gods were right next to it.

I picked it up.

It wasn't heavy. It wasn't odd. It was just a wooden box.

But I knew what was inside of it. Our future, our deaths.

Our freedom if we didn't screw this up.

"I'm gonna lift the lid," I said. "Abbi, keep those ears open."

She made a small humming noise.

I met Lula's gaze. She winked, and I huffed. "I'm just being cautious."

"You're always cautious," she said. "There's no way out of this but through. Open it."

A part of me—yeah, all of me—didn't want to do it. I wanted to put the box down and leave the book hidden away in this room forever.

To hell with Headwaters, gods, and all.

But Lula had lived a hundred years alone. I had lived a hundred years unable to touch her, to talk to her.

Because of Atë's monster, Headwaters.

Even though my gut said run, hide, do anything to

keep Lula far away from gods and their magic, I didn't step outside the circle. I stayed right there beside her.

"Then let's go," I said.

I opened the lid.

Lu sucked a quick breath, her pupils dilating like a predator spotting prey. The book was still wrapped in the kerchief Lula had wrapped it in back in Texas. Even so, it thrummed with an odd whispering musical chorus of magic.

"I'm going to pick it up and unlock it. Abbi?"

"Still quiet," she said.

"You hear the magic?" I asked her.

"No," Abbi said. "But it's quiet out there."

Lu pulled the book free and unwrapped it, dropping the handkerchief back into the box.

I expected…something. But the book was just a soft, tawny leather-bound book, slimmer than one would expect a gods' spell book would be, worked with gold threads and bits of stone and metal.

The carved bone lock was a bird in full dive, the loop of leather clutched in its talons.

Lu shifted her grip on the key, shaped like a wing, and inserted it into the lock.

She turned the key, and I heard the tick of tumblers sliding.

And then…

…and then the world filled with the scent of flowers. Sunlight burned the room to dust.

In the distance, a universe away, I heard Abbi whisper, "Oh no."

CHAPTER ELEVEN

The bakery was just as I remembered it, filled with warmth and the homey smell of bread and pies.

Tears pricked my eyes. I'd forgotten the shape of the place, how small it was, how the fresh white paint complemented the wood, how the old wooden floor shone.

Five round tables were placed strategically, allowing walking space between them.

Best of all, Lula was there beside me.

She gazed at the bakery with sorrow and desire, loneliness twisting her features.

Then she closed her eyes. "It's not real." Her voice shook.

"Of course it's real. It's yours. It's ours." I reached for her, but something was in the way. Something square and bulky in my arms.

The witch's box.

"It isn't. Can't be." Lula's eyes were still closed. "You need to refuse it, Brogan. This is a memory, a past we can't return to. This is an illusion. Close your eyes. We aren't here. We can't be. Not ever again. We're in New Mexico. With the Walches. With Abbi. With Cardamom."

It felt real, far more real than the hideout. It felt more real than the distant dream of our lives on the road.

I wanted to stay. But not without Lula.

"Fucking gods," I muttered.

Just before I closed my eyes, I saw Lula smile.

The smell of pine and copper filled my nose, and a chill washed over my skin. We were back, or at least I thought we were back, in the safe room.

"I'm going to open my eyes," Lula said. "Keep yours closed."

I didn't like that idea but did as she said. We were both winging it here, trying to feel our way through handling whatever the book was going to throw at us.

I counted heartbeats.

Finally, I heard Lu exhale. "Go ahead," she said. "We're in the safe room."

I opened my eyes. Lu stood directly in front of me, the book in her hands between us. The book wasn't even open, the key was still in the lock.

"How long were we gone?" I asked Abbi.

"You stayed right here," she said. "I didn't…did I miss a god? Did you get lost?"

"Not lost," Lula said. "The book just took us into a memory. A time we both miss."

She wasn't looking at me when she said it, so I shifted the box to one hand and touched her wrist.

Her gaze met mine. I was surprised to see tears there. She shook her head, telling me she was fine, and I gently cupped the side of her face.

"We don't need that time," I said. "We have all of our forever still ahead of us." I glanced over at Abbi who was standing just outside the circle, chewing on her bottom lip.

"All good, Pumpkin?"

"I don't hear anything. It's still quiet. I can't hear the book either. I didn't even know it did a magic."

"Think we got the proof we need?" I asked Lu. "That was big magic. The wards are holding."

"We haven't opened the book."

Yeah, that's what I figured she'd say.

"Let's do it then." I set the box down, but when I straightened, I held onto her wrist.

I didn't know what was going to happen, but I refused to let her go.

Lu steeled herself. I could feel the subtle shift in her muscles as she rocked just slightly to the balls of her feet, poised to respond to whatever the book was going to throw at us next.

"I'm going to open the cover."

I was nervous as hell, but that woman's hand didn't even tremble as she turned the key and opened the book.

The end pages were black and plain, but if I stared at them too long pinpricks of light flashed and faded. I heard distant voices screaming.

I blinked and the book looked like a book again, the voices silenced.

"Hell," I said. "The whole damn thing is a mind bend."

"It's…not easy to hold onto," Lula said.

"How?"

"It's moving. Can you see it moving?"

"No. Can you hear it? Did you see the lights?"

"No," she said. "Abbi?"

"Nothing. Quiet, quiet, quiet."

Well, I'd take that as a win.

"Can you turn the page?" I asked Lula. "Or is that a terrible idea?"

"Let's find out." She turned the page.

"There's nothing there," she said. "It's blank." She turned the next page. "It's blank. Brogan, there are no spells."

I heard her, I did. But I couldn't formulate the words to respond.

Because she was wrong. The pages were not blank.

They were filled with power, with galaxies, with microscopic wonders and mind-altering vistas twisting across plains of existence I couldn't comprehend.

I couldn't bear the horror and beauty of it, but I could not look away.

"Brogan!" Lula's voice drifted, distant and different.

Worried, I thought, *she's worried about me.*

But that thought was whisked into the river of power that twisted around me, a storm pulling apart and reshaping earth, stars, reality—and me.

"Brogan!"

A slap across my face rocked me back. The sting

bloomed and heated my cheek, bringing me back to the reality of her, the reality of now.

Lula had the book tucked under her arm, her gaze frantic. "Can you hear me?"

Her grip on my wrist was punishing, her fear sharp and overpowering.

I blinked and nodded, trying to orient.

I was in the hideout. In the safe room with Lula.

Abbi stood on tiptoes, ready to bolt out the door for help.

"My wrist," I said. "Love, my wrist."

Lu belatedly registered my words and relaxed her grip. "Jesus, Brogan. Are you…are you here? Are you hurt?"

"I think I'm okay. What happened? You hit me?"

She released my wrist. "You were just…you were just frozen, gone."

"You died!" Abbi shouted from outside of the circle. "Your soul was floating out and Lula couldn't catch it and I said slap you because you'd come back and you did and you *can't* die, Brogan." She wiped the inside of her arm over tears streaming down her face. "You can't."

Lula took my hand again, this time weaving her fingers with mine. "You can't," she agreed.

"I didn't mean to—I was lost. The spells. Lula, the power, the concepts, it's massive. I just…I don't know how anyone can wield that kind of magic."

She was nodding and nodding, tears gathering in her eyes.

"We put it away," she said. "Now."

I groaned, every joint and muscle complaining as I picked up the witch's box and held it open for her.

Lula locked the book, and placed it back in the box, her expression equal portions of hatred and fear.

I shut the box, and placed it on the floor again, in the center of the circle of sigils, the shadow cloth smothering out the voices, the images, the magic.

"I hate it," Lula whispered.

"I know."

She took my hand, holding on as if she were afraid I'd float away. We stepped outside the circle.

A wave of fatigue and vertigo hit me so hard, my knees went weak.

"Hold on," I said.

Lula didn't argue. She was trying to get her feet under her too.

I wasn't the only one affected by the book. But if just seeing the spells had nearly knocked my soul out of my bones, I couldn't imagine how hard it had been for her to hold it.

"Abbi," Lu asked, "did you hear anything? See any magic leaking beyond the room?"

"Nothing. The wards are really good." She crossed quickly to us and took Lula's other hand. "I think we should go now, though. I think we should go right now. I want cocoa. Do you think they have cocoa? We all need cocoa."

She dragged us to the door, and held it open, gently pushing Lu and me past her toward the hall.

Lorde was there, pacing. She whined and *woof*ed, sniffing Lula and me, and growling.

"It's okay," Lula knelt and rested her face against Lorde's fuzzy head.

Abbi shut the door. "Cookies too," she said, sniffing. "We all need lots of cookies."

"Lead the way, Pumpkin."

She glanced up at me. "You're going to follow, right?"

I touched the top of her head, her hair soft under my palm. "Of course, I am. I am not leaving you. Either of you."

She nodded, those eyes serious and ancient. Then she started down the hall. "Hado was worried," she said. "Hado says it's dinner time."

At the end of the hall a small meow called out.

"We're coming," Abbi said. "They're okay. They're still here." She bent to let Hado leap into her arms. "It was scary, but I wasn't afraid."

I touched Lu's shoulder. "We should eat."

She gave Lorde one last pet and stood.

"Do you think," she looked away, then met my gaze. "Do you think they'd have food for me?"

She was talking about blood. She never asked for blood. Holding the book had cost her more than I'd thought.

"Monster hunters? I'd expect they have some decent blood around here somewhere."

"I hate wanting it."

"I know. We're doing all sorts of hard things today. We're still standing."

The magic in the book had shaken me down to my

core. I couldn't fight it, couldn't outrun it or outthink it. I hadn't even known my spirit was leaving my body.

Dying.

Power like that shook a man.

We were walking in sync, and she rested her head against my shoulder, briefly.

"Don't you ever do that again," she whispered fiercely.

"We'll figure it out. Maybe it won't be so bad next time."

Even I didn't believe that.

I could see the argument in her, because it was in me too. Those spells weren't as bad as Cupid and Raven had said they were. They were worse.

The gods had said using the spells to kill Headwaters might kill us. They hadn't told us just opening the book would kick our butts.

I never wanted to see the inside of that damned book ever again.

"Hey," Pamela greeted us as we walked into the control room. "Abbi told us you opened the book. What do you need?"

Josie had a huge first-aid kit open on the table. Cardamom was leaning on the far wall watching us with eyes that caught more light than they should, his tattoos glowing softly against his skin.

"Food," I said, "to start with. Then advice, then sleep. Probably in that order."

"I'll get dinner off the stove," Pamela said. "Lula, do you need blood?"

Like I said, hunters were pros at this kind of thing.

"Yes," she said. "It doesn't have to be human."

"Got it. Give me a sec. Josie, a little help?"

"Sure." She latched up the kit and took it with her to the kitchen.

I pulled out a chair and dropped down at the table. I felt like I was carrying a fifty-pound bag of sand on my back.

Lula slipped into the chair beside me. Lorde settled under the table, her head on my foot.

"So," Cardamom said. "What did you do? Exactly."

"We opened the book," I said.

"I didn't sense the book, but you reek of god magic."

"It's in the safe room," Abbi said. She sat at the head of the table, Hado draped across her shoulders, her hair covering him so only his golden eyes could be seen. "I don't think any of the magic got out."

"It didn't." His tattoos flared, then dimmed. I wondered if he knew his magic was rolling over his skin. "What did you learn? What did the spells say?"

"I couldn't understand it enough to learn anything. It was…" I just shook my head. "No."

"Lula?"

"Blank pages. That's all I saw. I could feel the magic, but I couldn't see it, not a word."

He took a moment to process that, scowling.

"You are both very lucky it didn't permanently harm you. You can't guess your way through god power. And unless you agree that you won't touch the book again without me being there, and that you will *listen* to me, then our deal is off."

CHAPTER TWELVE

"Come on, Card." Pamela carried in a roast that smelled amazing and set it on a trivet in the middle of the long table. "They did what they did. We're all still breathing, the roof hasn't fallen in, and so far, there are no monsters at the door. I say we eat!"

She passed plates to me and Lula and Abbi, placed the rest by open chairs, then produced a goblet of what looked like red wine for Lu.

"This…I'm trying to keep you safe, right?" Card strolled over to the table. "Just promise you won't open the book again without me. Not until we find a way you can use it without it blowing out your brains."

"Next time we touch the book, you're there," I said. "Are we square? Because I'm starving and that smells like rosemary roast beef."

"Good nose," Josie swung into the room with more dishes. "Veggies and sides." She deposited several pots and bowls on the table. "Get it while it's hot."

Card hesitated, rubbing his thumb over his left wrist. Finally, he sat and took the plate Abbi offered him.

"Thank you, Pamela, Josie. And thank you Brogan. Lula?" he asked. "Does Brogan's promise cover you?"

She ran a discrete finger over her lips which were stained red from the blood she'd sipped. "I won't touch the book unless you are there, Cardamom, at least while you are helping us."

"Only then?" He scooped a rich yellow rice dish onto his plate. It smelled divine.

"You're not going to be there when we face Headwaters."

"Won't I?"

"You're only here until we figure out how to use the book," she said.

"No. I'm here to use every trick I can to keep you both alive when you use the book. Especially when you confront Headwaters."

Lu opened her mouth, shut it, then frowned.

"Josie, this is delicious," he said. "You're right. The spice is spot on."

"Even with the extra dill?" she teased.

"I stand corrected."

I helped myself to a portion of beef, vegetables, bread, rice, and the salad was passed my way. Lula put some of the cooked vegetables on her plate and drizzled them with the broth. I slid a piece of buttered bread over to her.

"Homemade. You'll love it with the yam."

She flashed me a small smile, pleased I'd added to

her meal. She didn't eat much, didn't have to. But I'd fallen into an old habit.

Back in the day when we'd both been alive and mortal, I used to add a little of my food onto her plate all the time.

She dutifully tried the bread with the yam and her eyelids fluttered.

"Told you it was good," I said around a mouthful.

"Family recipe," Pamela said. "It's the nutmeg that brings it all together."

"And the butter," Josie said.

"Always the butter," Pamela agreed.

"Compliments to the chefs," I said.

Food made everything seem a little better with the world, and when Pamela suggested coffee, I took her up on it. So did Cardamom. Abbi asked for cocoa, and Lu wandered into the kitchen with Pamela, Josie, and Abbi to decide on a tea.

"Want to talk about it?" Card placed a cup of coffee in front of me and settled back in his seat.

He'd helped stack plates and had taken them to the sink. Josie had chased him out with the coffee, pointedly telling him she had a specific way she liked the dishwasher loaded.

I could hear Lu talking with Pamela and Josie, and the sudden sound of her soft laughter meant the world to me.

"The book?" I asked.

"That. Any of it. The gods. The magic you've dealt with. The back-to-life thing. I've been targeted—am still a target—of powerful people. I know it's frustrating. Terrifying."

I grunted. "You got a couple years? Because that's how long it'll take to cover it all."

"Maybe just the highlights."

I thought it over. "Some of the gods want the book hidden."

"Cupid?"

"He's one of them. Some gods want control of it."

"Atë?"

"And Mithra. And, apparently, Apep."

He whistled. "Mithra is no one to fuck with. Atë's only goal is to cause misery to anyone who crosses her path—the gods in particular."

"I am aware."

"But Apep…He's your worst problem. That god crushes galaxies without a thought. If he wants the book…"

He took a swig of his coffee, then leaned his elbows on the table, suddenly all business.

"Tell me what happened when you opened the book."

"Lula opened it. I can't touch it. She flipped through the pages."

"What spells did you see?"

"I couldn't…" I stopped to gather my thoughts. "It wasn't like a list of words, or a recipe. I saw concepts, power twisted into theories, magic forced into methods beyond my understanding."

"You saw more than one page?"

"I think so."

"Think?"

"I lost track."

"Which means?"

"Abbi said my soul left my body."

"Ah." He sat back and drank again. "It's *that* kind of power. Don't worry, I didn't expect it to be easy, we'll find a way into it. Could you see any words at all?"

"No."

"That's where we'll focus. What about Lula?"

"What about her?"

"Did the book fight her? Was holding it heavy? Did it freeze, burn, try to fly out of her hands?"

"I don't know. Lu?"

She stepped out of the kitchen. At her smile, my heart beat double time.

"I was listening." She sat next to me, the cup of tea —mint and licorice—cupped between her palms.

"Tell me what happened when you held it," Card said. "Was it heavy or hot? Did it try to escape your grip?"

She frowned, as if trying to drag up old memories. "At first, it just seemed like a book. When I unlocked it, the pages were blank. There was nothing on them."

"There was," I said. "There is."

"Not that I could see. But after I turned the pages, it was…I don't know how to explain it. It was aware of me. Like I wasn't holding a book, but instead some kind of…intelligence. Some kind of creature. It did not like being trapped."

The silence stretched out.

I wasn't sure how to respond. In the very brief

encounters I'd had with the book, it had lashed out and quickly put me in my place. I'd always sensed a kind of awareness in it. But an intelligence?

"Do you think there is something living trapped in there?" Card asked like this was a normal thing to discuss over after-dinner coffee. "A soul, a demon, a god?"

"For fuck's sake," I groaned. "That's just what we need."

Lu shook her head. "It's not…I can't fit it into a category that makes any sense. I've never felt anything like it before, and I've been around a lot of magical items."

"Good enough. I'll see what comes up in research. Ricky has the Crossroads looking into everything it can find about the book. I have a few sources I can ask. The Walches offered their library and archives. If nothing turns up, we'll proceed with ample caution."

"When do you want to start?"

"Tomorrow," I said. Lu huffed a breath, then nodded.

"After we rest." She brushed my knee under the table.

"Good. That gives me tonight to prepare." He stood. "I'll get going. Good-night, Gauges. Don't touch the book without me."

I gave him a half-hearted salute. He grinned and disappeared into the kitchen.

He exchanged a few words with the women in there and left with a fresh cup of coffee and a thermos. He took the stairs up and disappeared into one of the rooms filled with books.

"The book's alive, huh?" I asked.

Lu shifted to sit sideways, propping her feet onto my legs. I twisted from the table to give her more room.

"That's as close as I can explain it," she said. "You saw things but not words? How do we cast spells without words?"

"Hell if I know. But next time I'll be ready for it."

She nodded quickly. "So will I. It fought me. When I saw what it was doing to you…I closed it. But it fought me."

"Marvelous. Like the spells aren't hard enough to deal with, we have to fight the book too."

"With Card's help, maybe next time will be different."

"It will be!" Card's voice floated down from above.

That made me smile. "Apparently it isn't only moon rabbits who have big ears around here. You want to take this somewhere private?"

"Does it involve a shower and bed?"

"Only the best for you, my love."

Abbi popped back into the room. "Are you going somewhere?"

"Just to bed," I said.

"Shower and bed," Lu corrected. "Josie said the water pressure is wonderful."

Abbi tipped her head, listening for something. "Card is upstairs doing magic?"

"Preparation and research," I said.

"I'm going to watch him."

"Don't stay up too late," I said, even though she wasn't really a child and I wasn't her father.

Her smile was huge. "I like the night. I might stay up *all* night!"

Lorde paced out from under the table, stretching and yawning. She stopped next to Lula.

"Who's staying up all night?" Elmer asked. He'd stashed his gun but still had his hat and jacket on. He looked a little dusty and smelled of the desert night.

"I am!" Abbi said.

"You two turning in?"

"Thought so," I said. "The wards holding?"

"Quiet as a mouse out there. Not sure if I like it, but it beats the alternative. We're good for now. Get sleep while you can."

"Grandpa?" Pamela called out. "You back? I put a plate aside for you."

Elmer patted his stomach. "Gotta take care of this. See you in the morning, then." He strolled into the kitchen.

Abbi had already tiptoed to the stairs and was sneaking up them, pausing to listen to whatever it was Card was doing up there.

Lu touched my arm and started down the hall. "You think we're actually going to fall asleep?"

"No. Worth trying, though." A huge yawn ruined my statement.

The shower at the end of the hall was locker room style with three shower stalls and clean towels folded on the open shelf.

I locked the door, and Lu started the shower.

"More than one shower." I pulled off my boot, unlaced the other.

"We only need one." She eased out of her overshirt, then unbuckled her belt. She stowed the knives while I stripped out of shirt and pants.

Lula's gaze took in every inch of my body, her scrutiny clinical.

"I'm fine," I said.

"Bruised." She pointed to my thigh, my low back, my shoulder, my wrist.

"Still fine. You're bruised too, love."

She shrugged but glanced at her body. "Not as bad as you."

"Well," I walked toward the water which was radiating steam now, "I don't heal as fast as you."

I ducked under the stream and moaned. The water pressure *was* wonderful, the temperature perfect. Lula ran her hand down my back. I shivered at her touch, and turned, welcoming her into the spray.

We stood there for a long time, savoring the sensation, the comfort, the safety of being in each other's arms, water falling over us, and washing us clean.

Eventually, Lula reached for the soap, and then we set to the business of scrubbing the dirt, blood, and sweat down the drain.

While our touches were gentle and loving, neither of us had the energy to take it further than that.

I regretfully turned off the spigot, and we dried ourselves, then wrapped into the robes folded next to the towels.

I shuffled into the bedroom, rubbing my eyes and yawning.

Lula handed me a clean pair of shorts. She slipped into a tank and loose pants.

"Go ahead." She pressed her hand against my hip to encourage me to the bed. "I'll lock the door and turn out the light."

I aimed toward the bed and dropped into it like a rock.

The light flicked off, filling the room with calm and dark.

Lula slipped onto the bed, drawing the blankets up and turning toward me.

"It's going to be okay," she said.

"I know." We were both lying, but the comfort behind the words was real.

"Brogan," she said after a moment.

I dragged myself back from the edge of sleep. "Mmmm?"

"It isn't…it's harder than I thought."

"The book?" I mumbled.

But she didn't have a chance to answer.

Red light snapped on and flooded the room, a klaxon shattering the air.

"Breach!" Elmer's voice echoed down the hallway. "We've been breached."

CHAPTER THIRTEEN

Someone had killed the klaxon, but the control room was still flooded with red light.

I'd thrown on a shirt, pants, and shoes, as had Lula. Everyone was gathered in the smaller room with the security screens, scanning for the danger.

"Can you tell which ward was tripped?" Card asked. He had pulled on a hoodie that smothered the tattoos on his skin, though the stone and wood amulet hanging from a cord around his neck glowed a deep green.

"East," Elmer pointed at a screen which showed nothing but sand, rocks, and black sky.

"Did you see what tripped it?" Lula asked.

Pamela sat at the desk below the screens. She tapped keys and one of the screens went blank, then snapped back to life.

"This is right before the alarm went off."

I leaned forward trying to make out anything on the screen.

But there was nothing. No movement whatsoever.

"I don't—" I started.

The screen flashed white, then crackled with static and went dead.

"Well, shit," Elmer said. "Power, not form."

"Power?" I asked. "God power?"

Card shook his head, then stopped. "Maybe. I'll go out and see."

"You'll do no such thing," Josie said. "This here," she pointed at our feet. "Secure. Out there you'd just get picked off or used as a hostage. We stay in the fortress to defend the fortress and everyone in it. Understand? No heroes."

"All right," Card said. "Then how do we find out what's out there?"

"Maybe we don't?" Abbi said. "If we're quiet, maybe it will just leave?"

I put my hand on her shoulder, and she leaned into my leg. She was a powerful deity and very brave, but she was also the first to choose flight or hiding as a survival tactic.

"We sent a scout," Elmer said.

"What happened to stay in the fortress to defend the fortress?" Card asked.

"Scout was already out there," Pamela said. "We should be hearing from it soon."

Lu shifted her stance, hands falling on the hilts of her daggers. Lorde stood next to her, panting and silent, her furry ears pricked up into triangles.

Even Hado had shifted from his little kitten form into the shape of a large black panther silently pacing the room behind us.

Time ticked by while we watched the screens.

Pamela pointed. "All right. Scout's coming this way."

I didn't see anything on the screen, but Elmer pivoted. "I'll see him in."

Card watched him go. "Any reason why someone shouldn't follow him?"

"On it," Josie said. "We shouldn't have a problem, because nothing can get through the door Scout's gonna use, but good call on the paranoid caution, Wizard." She jogged out of the room to catch up with Elmer.

"Weather's picking up," Pamela said.

Lightning popped across the sky, serpent quick, a huge roll of thunder breaking through the silence.

We were buried a good distance underground. I didn't want to think about how loud that had to have been to reach us this far down.

"That's not a storm," Abbi said. "It's a god."

"Thor?" Lula asked.

Abbi shook her head.

Card wrapped his hand around the amulet and closed his eyes for a moment. Light glowed through the sleeves of his hoodie.

"Not Thor," he said. "That is a dark, chaotic power."

"Atë?" I asked.

"I don't think so."

"Apep?" Lula asked.

We hadn't seen the god of chaos yet, though the hunters said he was on our tail.

"I'd need to use stronger magic to know, and right

now, I think it's a bad idea to draw that kind of attention our way."

"Yeah, let's not do that," Pamela agreed.

The screens whited out and thunder roared, loud enough, I wanted to cover my ears.

"*Wow*," Abbi mouthed.

It was maybe five minutes later when Josie called out from the other room.

"All clear?"

"Steady on," Pamela called back.

Josie strode into the room. "Scout says it's god power, thinks it's Apep. But the god isn't near. This is a remote scan."

"So, a sweep to see if anything pings," Pamela said.

"Likely."

"Not sure I want to bet my life on likely," I said.

"We'll wait it out, see if he takes his storm and moves on," Elmer said, stepping back into the room. "Or if he wants to make trouble."

The minutes ticked by. I counted the seconds between the flashes of lightning and thunder, my gaze glued to the screens. At first, it seemed the storm was stationed above us, refusing to leave.

Then a huge wind picked up and rain fell in sheets. It was impossible, but I thought I heard ravens calling over the storm.

The lightning crackled toward the west. Thunder thumped and exploded, like bombs punching through the sky to shake the horizon, moving farther and farther away with each strike.

The time between flash and bang grew longer. The storm whipped and raged, but it was shifting, moving.

"I think we're in the clear," Pamela said. "Anyone? Card? Abbi?"

Card had pushed his sleeves up so he could clasp his wrists. The glow of his quiescent magic seeped through his fingers.

"Again, I'd need magic to know for sure, but that power is moving past us. West."

"I don't hear the god anymore," Abbi said. "He… wasn't here. Not physically. He was just looking."

"Hell," I breathed. If that was "just looking" I didn't want anything to do with the god actually finding us.

"Will that attract more gods?" Josie asked. "Now that one's been sniffing around the place?"

Abbi shook her head, then stopped. "I don't know. The other gods are helping keep us hidden. Cupid. Raven."

"If Apep knew we were here," Lu said, "we'd know."

She was right.

Elmer tapped on the doorframe. "Scout says he's moved on. For now."

"You trust this scout?" Card asked.

"Sure do."

I caught the skitter of a little brown lizard disappearing behind a shelf in the corner of the room. I couldn't be sure it was Sniffer, who had vetted Card outside earlier today, but I had a feeling that was who the scout was.

Card's head jerked toward the corner. "Do you smell dragon?"

"Dragons? Down here? Can't see how that's likely," Elmer said. "It's getting on late. I'll monitor the screens. Everyone else, get some sleep if you can."

He pressed his steady hand on Pamela's shoulder, and she glanced up at him.

"You sure?" she asked. "I'm good for a couple hours."

"You can spell me then."

She stood and Josie reached for her.

"Not that I think I'm gonna sleep," Pamela said. "Nothing like a brush with a god to get the old heart pumping."

"Once you hit the pillow, you'll be out cold." Josie tugged her toward the door and out of the room. "Night all. See you in a few hours."

"You sleeping?" I asked Card.

He was still staring at the corner where the lizard had disappeared, but he shook his head. "I don't need much sleep. Besides, I still have some research I want nailed down before we address the book."

"I'm staying up!" Abbi announced. "Come on, Hado, let's find new places to hide."

She leaned into my leg again, almost like a sideways hug without arms, then bounced out of the room, Hado a huge shadowy panther prowling behind her.

"I know she's spying on me," Card said.

I checked how I should take that and was relieved by his smile.

"I don't mind," he went on. "But I just wanted to

say, again, I'm here to help you with the book. I don't want the cursed thing. I don't want to use it. I have my own problems, believe me."

"We heard you've made some enemies," I said. "Wizards?"

"Wizards. Not the same kind of problem as gods, but…not great."

"Do we need to keep an eye out for wizards now?" Elmer asked.

"No. I've been careful about my movements and magic," Card said. "The Crossroads has protections set up for me. Ricky's staked claims that would trigger all sorts of laws and conflicts if the wizards try to push it. For now, for once, I'm not the person in the most trouble."

"You say that like it's an unusual thing," Lu said.

"It's rare." This time the wizard's smile was brilliant and filled with the sort of wickedness I last saw on the trickster god's face. "People don't tend to find ways to piss off powerful people as often as I do."

"You're in good company, son," Elmer said.

Card started toward the door. "Just remember, I'm here to help. Nice dragon kind, by the way."

Elmer swore under his breath and picked up a thermos on the floor next to the desk. "Thinks he's so smart." He unscrewed the stopper and poured coffee into the silver lid. "You Gauges staying up like the other two?"

"No," I said. "We're going to bed."

"Elmer," Lula said, "thank you—again—for this place. For putting your own safety on the line for us."

He swiveled the chair, making it creak. "Family looks after family." It was a mantra, a ritual. "It's a heavy burden that's fallen on your shoulders. Your choices are going to change the world for all of us.

"Giving a little of what we have to help you is the least we can do. I'll keep an eye out now. You two kids get some rest."

I snorted at the "kids" comment. I hadn't been a kid for almost a hundred years. Both of us were older than he was, in fact.

But Lula tugged on my hand, and there would never be a time I wouldn't follow her.

"From the top," Card said. "Easy now."

The wizard perched on a wooden chair—he'd specifically said he needed a wooden chair and had inspected all of the chairs in the hideout before settling on this one.

He was outside the circle of spells, in the west corner —again, he'd insisted on that—with a bark-bound book on the table beside him. The table also held several candles in a variety of colors, a bowl of water, and a cup of tea.

I didn't know what all the other stuff was for, but the tea was for drinking.

Lu and I hadn't slept deeply, but I'd drifted off for at least an hour or two and felt better for it.

I was sporting a low headache from the bump on the head I'd taken yesterday, and all the aches and bruises were making themselves known, but the hearty meal and about half a pot of coffee had set me up in a better state all around.

Even Lu had eaten—fruit and bread with honey—and Abbi, of course, had nearly demolished an entire tray of cinnamon buns.

Abbi wandered about in the safe room, careful of the sigils on the floor, Hado in kitten form draped across her shoulders.

Lorde wasn't in the room, because we didn't want her to get hurt, so she was currently sleeping with the toys and bones Pamela and Josie had showered on her.

Elmer turned in for sleep right after breakfast. Pamela, Josie, and the lizard were holding down the fort.

On Card's suggestion, Lu and I were both wearing comfortable clothes, and we'd brought blankets, pillows, a first-aid kit, and (worryingly) a fire extinguisher into the room. All of them were stacked in a corner.

"Since the book needs both of you to work with it, I want you both to step into the spell circle at the same time," Card said, his voice falling easily into a teacher's patient, upbeat tone.

"All right," I said. "Three, two, one."

Lu and I both stepped inside the protective circle.

"No fire, no smoke, no ancient horrors bursting through the walls," Card said. "I like this. Great start."

I'd like to say he was joking, just keeping it light, but I had a feeling he was dead serious.

Breakfast sat heavily in my gut, and sweat trickled down my pits and spine.

Fear, I thought, clenching and unclenching my fists.

Every instinct in me said I should run. Grab Lula, Abbi, and Card, and shove all of us out of the room.

Wild images of locking the witch's box in chains, of burying it beneath the stone floor, of pumping concrete into the safe room to contain and hide the book for good, whipped through my mind.

I wanted out of here. I wanted us all out of here.

But that choice wasn't mine. Even if I could talk Lula into not trying to use the book (an option I knew was hopeless, but which I wasn't entirely giving up on, either), we still had to take it somewhere safe.

Leaving it here wasn't an option. The hunters couldn't keep the gods from finding it, no matter how protected their hideaway might be.

It had to be taken to Ordinary. And Lula and I were the only two people who could attempt it.

I understood the logic of the situation we were in. But my self-preservation instincts were howling.

I wiped a palm over my mouth, scratching at the sweat in my beard.

Lu threw me a concerned look. I shook my head.

We'd had our talk before breakfast. I wanted us to find another weapon. She wanted to use the book.

I'd lost the argument (again). I wouldn't be able to talk her out of this until we had given this whole spell-casting thing a real, concerted, guided effort.

That didn't make me want to toss my breakfast any less.

Just knowing she was going to open the book, and that I'd have to consume the magic, those concepts, and try to read it, made me want to set the thing on fire.

Maybe that was why Card had insisted we bring a fire extinguisher.

Lu tugged the shadow cloth off of the witch's box. Card made an impressed sound.

"That cloth is brilliant. The box is too. I can't sense the book at all."

"Told you," Abbi said.

"Witches?" he asked.

"Witches made the box," I said, trying to control my breathing. The book whispered, leaves shivering under winter's hand. "Cloth was loaned by the hunters."

"They have quite the stash of things tucked away in this place," he said. "Can't imagine they got it all on the up and up. Which I approve of. How are you doing, Brogan?"

"Me? Fit as a fiddle." I couldn't seem to get my words and breathing lined up.

"You're panicked, which is to be expected."

Lula raised an eyebrow and took a minute to size me up.

"Who are you going to believe? Me or the wizard?"

"I can feel your nerves from here," he said, like I'd been talking to him. "As I said, I would be more worried if you were perfectly calm."

"We'll take it slow," Lula said. "We'll be careful."

"We?" I asked, trying to smile. "Not sure 'careful' is a state you and I have ever visited."

"This is a good time to try it."

Her concern, Card's attention, and even Abbi, chewing on her bottom lip and looking worried, made me fill my lungs and exhale slowly.

"I'm fine, I'm fine. Just a little spooked from yesterday. I can do this."

To prove it, I bent and picked up the witch's box.

Maybe it was the storm last night, or hearing Lula say holding the book was like holding a living thing, but, well, it felt like something was alive in that box.

Something that wanted out.

"So far so good," Card said. "Just hold it there a minute, Brogan. I want to set some wards of my own. Abbi?"

"I can help." She pulled her mortar and pestle from wherever she kept them.

Card said something to her I couldn't make out. She nodded and walked in the opposite direction around the room, pausing at each corner to do something with the powder in the mortar.

"Still good?" I asked Lu.

"It's the same as yesterday," she said. "I know it's in there. I'm sure it knows I'm out here. But I don't feel…malice?"

"Don't tell me you're gonna start trusting it."

"No. I'm just not planning to get in a battle with it either. Not if I don't have to. If we were made to use the book, to wield those spells, I don't see why it would want to fight us."

"That's done." Card came around to stand at our side, outside the circle. "We've put up support for the wards, added cushioning. Dampeners for explosions and stray magic."

"Not sure explosion was on my bingo card," I grumbled.

Card grinned. The tattoos on his bare arms and up his neck glowed. "This is magic training, Brogan. There's bound to be some kind of exhilarating moments. Which is why we've padded the room. I promise you. This is safer than most places where I've trained."

"Guy who gets powerful people mad at him? Not sure you're the shining example you think you are."

"Says the man who gets powerful *gods* mad at him," Card noted. "Plus, you have no idea what kind of power I've dealt with before."

His eyes, usually a brilliant green, were shot with flickering fire.

I was beginning to wonder where, exactly, he fell in the powerful hierarchy of the wizard ranks. With that kind of response, I notched him up a few tiers.

"Remember," he went on, the amenable teacher once again. "I just need you to hold it and turn the pages. Brogan, you're going to keep your mouth shut. Just put on the glasses—you still have the glasses, don't you?"

I shifted my hold on the box and drew the glasses out of my shirt pocket.

They were made of bronze, silver, and gold. Card had been working on them most of the night.

"Go ahead and put those on," he said. I slid the glasses into place.

The room looked exactly the same. So did Lula, Card, and Abbi, but Card assured me the glasses were built with magic that would allow him to see some of what I was seeing.

"Are they working?" I asked.

Card hummed. "We'll know as soon as Lula opens the book. So, are you both ready? Remember, Lu, you just need to hold it and turn the page. Brogan, no talking. Just look at the page. Got it?"

"Yes," I said.

Lu nodded, her gaze steady on me. "I'm taking it out of the box."

She opened the box. She pulled the book out, and unlike yesterday, she was moving slowly and treating it like it was made of glass. Explosive glass.

"Got it?" I asked.

"Got it."

I put the box on the floor, then didn't know what to do with my hands. I wanted to touch her, to brace my hands under hers to carry the weight of the book, but I didn't dare brush the cover.

"Card?" Lula asked.

"I'm right here," he said. "I see it. Go ahead."

Lula unlocked the book and opened it. I braced myself for the song, for the power and the magic and the tidal wave of concepts and clashing realities.

Instead, I saw a page with symbols burning in soft yellow light.

"That's not how it was," I said.

"Things change," Card said. "There could have been a trigger spell to ward people off. If so, that's done, and we're into uncharted water. Even if not, the book is sentient enough, it might be on to us. It might know we're here to find a spell that will help us get rid of one of the gods who wants to possess it and use it poorly."

I figured he was talking for our benefit and also (weirdly) for the book's.

"Can you read that?" I asked Card.

"It's an opening screed. Not a spell. The god who wrote it is not lost."

"That's a lot of expertise all of a sudden, Card," Lula said.

"I'm good at magic," he said matter-of-factly. "Yay, for me. Let's take advantage of it."

"Turn the page?" Lula asked.

"Yep," I said.

She did. The symbols here were violet and looked like holes burned into the universe.

"Keep going. Not a lost god," Card said.

Lu turned the page again.

"Is this it?" Abbi asked. "Is this all we're going to do?"

"What did you think we were going to do?" Card asked.

"The magic. Trying it. Letting it loose."

"Oh, they'll try it," Card said. "But not until we think we've found a spell that won't kill us or destroy half the world. Preferably a spell written by a lost god."

Lu turned the page. It seemed to disappear as soon as it was turned, leaving behind the scent of crushed rosemary and sorrow.

"Lu?" I asked.

"I'm okay," she said, but I could see her hands were beginning to shake. She turned the page.

"Step back!" Card yelled.

We both jumped backward.

Something lashed out of the book, snapping and wailing, then was gone.

"Holy shit," I said. "Card?"

"Not a lost god spell." He didn't sound the least bit fazed, the jerk. "Let's do five more and take a break."

"You okay?" I asked Lu.

She nodded, her breathing a little fast.

"Five more," she said.

"Five," I said.

She turned the page. A shower of wind chimes and bleached bones sang out ancient curses.

"Four."

She turned the next page.

The flash of light was blinding.

I yelled, Card shouted, and Lula jerked backward, the book tumbling to the stone floor.

CHAPTER FOURTEEN

"Brogan?" she asked.

"Can't see," I said. "Give me a minute." I pulled the glasses off and rubbed the back of my hand over my eyes. I shivered, even though it was sweltering. "Are you hurt?"

"No. I dropped the book. I'm not going to pick it up yet, so don't step forward. It's close to your feet."

Her hand rested on my arm. I pulled her to me in an awkward hug.

"You okay, Card? Abbi?" I called out, my arms around Lula, both of us shaking.

"Card is lying down," Abbi said. "But I'm okay. The room is okay. I don't hear anything bad outside."

"I'm fine," Card said, his voice coming from somewhere near the floor. "I just need to catch my breath."

"We need a break," I said.

"Card said five. We have three more pages," Lu said, not moving an inch away from me.

"Maybe we need a snack?" Abbi asked.

"I can do three," Card said. "Brogan?"

My sight was returning from the edges inward, as if I'd stared too long at the sun.

"Not until I can see," I said. "But, yes."

Lu nodded against my chest.

Abbi made encouraging noises, helping Card back to the chair and getting his tea. My throat was dry as if I'd been talking non-stop. I could drink a gallon of water, but we'd all agreed bringing food or drink inside this protected circle spell space was a terrible idea.

"Okay," I said, "I can see. Just three and we take a break. Yes?"

"Yes," Lula agreed.

She leaned away but held my forearms so she could study my face. "How many fingers?" she asked holding up her hand.

"Five. But you're holding up two."

She smiled briefly. There were shadows under her eyes, shadows that hadn't been there this morning. Holding the book, turning the pages was taking more of a toll on her than she was admitting.

"Three pages," I repeated.

"I know," she said. "Are you ready, Card?"

"I am. Brogan, put the glasses back on first. Let me see if they are damaged."

I did. "Good?"

"Good. Lula?"

"I'm picking up the book." She held it carefully in her hands and squared off in front of me. "I'm opening the cover."

I nodded, took a deep breath. I had no idea how far

we'd gotten into the book, but somehow Lula did. She opened the cover and several pages at the same time. The page she opened too was not one I'd seen before.

"Three," I said.

A soft wind brushed across my skin, and moonlit petals filled the space.

"Nice," Card said, "but not a lost god spell."

"Two."

Lu turned the page. There were words there, all of them squirming and thrashing like worms caught in a blow torch.

"No," Card said.

"One," I said.

Lu turned the page.

The page was covered from corner to corner in black ink, the words written in a tight, precise script.

No other magics or sensations radiated off of the page. It just looked like ink on paper.

"Break time," I said.

"No," Card's voice was thready with excitement. "Stay there. Don't close the book. I think that might be what we're looking for."

Lu looked up at me. "Can you read it?"

I focused on the text. It wasn't a language I'd ever seen before, but I knew how it would sound if I spoke each word.

"I can. I think so. I don't know what it says, though. Don't know what kind of spell it is. Card, you got some insight on this?"

"I can't see god power attached to it. Not active. I

can't sense the god who made it. This is a lost god spell. I think it is."

"Think?" Lu and I said at the same time.

"I know magic," he said, "but I've never seen a spell from a lost god. But this…this could be it."

"How do we know?" Abbi asked. "How do we know for sure?"

"Brogan and Lula cast it," Card said.

The silence was unsettling, then I couldn't help it, I snorted. "Fuck. All right. I need a drink of water first, and another cup of coffee. Lu, do you think you can find this page again?"

"I can."

"Let's put it back in the box."

She closed and locked the book and put it in the box. I shut the lid and draped the cloaking cloth over it.

"Step out at the same time," Card said.

We did so. I shivered like I'd just crawled out of the storm into a warm house.

"You did it!" Abbi bounded over to us. "You found the spell!"

"We found *a* spell," I said. "Still don't know if it's the one we need."

"I'll consult with Ricky, the Crossroads, and a few books I have there." Card was already headed to the door. "I should be able to figure out what the spell is meant to do."

He waved his hand across the door, releasing the wards he had set before stepping out.

"That was good," Abbi said. "You did really good."

She beamed up at Lula and me. "I bet it is the spell you need."

"Are you just saying that because you're bored and don't want us to go through the rest of the book page by page?" Lu asked.

"Yes," she said simply. "That book is too much… everything. The power and magic…" She shook her head. "I want that spell to be the right spell."

"So do I," I said. But I had a gut feeling it was not the right spell. There was nothing about it that made it seem powerful enough to kill a god-created monster. There was no sense of violence in it.

If anything, it felt blank, empty, as if it were nothing more than a laundry list written in plain ink.

We closed the door behind us, Lu tugging to make sure the latch was set.

Lorde trotted down the hallway, her tail wagging.

Abbi let go of my hand and jogged to meet her. "We found a spell, Lordey. It might be the right spell, too." She petted Lorde's back then jumped off to the control room.

"It's not the right spell, is it?" Lu asked.

"I don't know. The first lost god spell we find in the book just happens to be the right one?" I asked. "How often does a coincidence like that go our way?"

"More often than it does for other people," she said. "With all the forces and powers and magic messing with our lives? It could be the right spell because Fate decided we're going to find it now."

"I'd like to stay well beneath the notice of her or any other gods."

"If wishes were horses," she said.

"Then beggars would ride."

It was an old nursery rhyme. I was surprised I remembered it.

We strolled into the control room.

Pamela was reading on a screen. She looked up. "Snacks in the kitchen," she said. "Fresh drinks, coffee and tea if you want it."

"I'm getting a drink, you want anything?" I asked Lu.

"Tea?"

"Earl Grey?"

"Please."

She pulled out a chair and sat, propping her boots up on the opposite chair. "Any movement outside?"

"All quiet," Pamela said. "Grandpa did another check on the perimeter. We're snug as bugs."

"Scout still out there?"

I didn't hear her reply once I pushed through the doors into the kitchen. Abbi was (surprisingly) not there, but evidence of her strafing run was clear in the huge slice of pumpkin pie that was missing and the half-empty marshmallow bag.

I found the mugs, started the kettle for Lu, and turned on the tap for a glass of water, which I downed in one go and refilled.

I poured coffee, thinking I might go for a snack of the cheeses, smoked meats, and nuts they'd set out, when I heard Lu's phone ring.

It wasn't loud, but it was a silly little tune that managed to carry, even over other noise.

Lots of people might be calling her—Ricky, for one. Raven, because he was like that. Maybe even Dot from the B&B back in Illinois.

But I knew from the chill that shot through my bones, it was none of those people.

Whoever was on the phone was not a friend.

I barged into the control room.

Lu was on her feet, facing me, but from the look on her face, she didn't see me.

Pamela was on her feet too, but she leaned over her tablet, her fingers flying.

"Speaker," I said. "Lu, put it on speaker."

She snapped out of her daze and put her phone down, turning on the speaker function.

Insipid orchestral music played. The caller must have put Lu on hold.

"Who is it?" I asked.

"Headwaters," Lu whispered. She swallowed and scowled, color coming back to her cheeks. "His secretary put me on hold."

"Why?"

"Because Headwaters wants to talk to me. Directly."

"He knows," I said. "Knows we're on to him."

Card came down the stairs, moving silently, a book open in his hand, his tattoos glowing softly.

The music stopped and a woman's voice said, "Headwaters will speak with you now."

A click sounded, and I knew something evil hovered on the other side of the connection. An evil we'd been hunting for decades.

"Lula Gauge," a slow, low male voice said. "I know you have the spell book of the gods."

My heart hammered so loudly, I could barely hear his words. This felt like a nightmare. One where I was locked in place. Frozen.

Lu's breathing was fast, both rage and fear. But her voice when she spoke was calm and without inflection.

"We will find you," she said. "And we will kill you."

The pause on the other end was long. I couldn't tear my gaze away from the phone screen, Lula didn't move.

It felt like not even a single grain of time fell.

"You know what I am? Who I am?"

"Yes."

"Then you know that if I had wanted to kill you, all these long years, I could have ended you in an instant. Wiped you off this earth. You and spirit-out-of-spirit, Brogan."

"Atë wouldn't allow it," Lu said.

Headwaters made a considering noise. "Not all gods are powerful," he said. "Nor do all gods remain in control of the power they think they have. You have the book."

"Meet me and I'll tell you."

It wasn't a laugh. But it was a sound that conveyed humor—and derision.

"And kill me, I presume."

"Meet. Me."

"Do you think you have power? Over me? You are nothing. You cannot kill me. No weapon can. Gods themselves have built me, and only gods can tear me down."

"Name the place," she said, "and we'll find out."

"Bring me the spell book of the gods. Or I will no longer find you useful alive."

That, the overwhelming statement of bravado was what finally snapped me out of it.

I broke a hard sweat, but adrenalin still pumped through me. Headwaters was like every other god and creature we'd run across.

He wanted the spell book of the gods.

And he couldn't use it without us.

"Where?" Lu asked. "When?"

"Tomorrow, dawn. The Continental Divide."

Lu's gaze flicked up to me. She wasn't asking for my opinion. She was warning me she wasn't going to say no.

"Dawn." She thumbed off the phone.

"Call was from out of state," Pamela said. "I'm going to say it's a burner phone. That was his—" she looked over at Lu, "—his? voice."

"Does he know where we are?" Card asked. "Can he have pinpointed this place through the call?"

"No. You would not even believe the magical redirects we have. He might know you're in New Mexico. Probably why he suggested the Continental Divide."

"We don't have much time," Lu said. "We have to try that spell."

"You're not seriously thinking of meeting that monster at dawn?" Card asked.

"I am dead serious we are going to kill that monster at dawn." Her eyes were narrow, and I caught a flash of her sharp canines.

Fury that burned for nearly a hundred years did not fade. No, for Lula, for me, it became a concentrated, explosive inferno.

But using the book to kill Headwaters when we could barely hold it, could barely read it, was madness.

"We need to talk," I said. "Lula, you and I need to talk."

"No," she said. "We need to work. I know you don't want to use the book. You've told me that over and over. But I am not going to let your fear get in the way of me killing that monster. You have to just deal with it right now, Brogan. There is no more time for you to be afraid. There's no turning back. We kill Headwaters tomorrow *with the book.*"

She wasn't yelling, but her voice was loud. Hard.

"Of course I'm afraid," I said. "I'd be a fool not to be. Use your head, Lula. We aren't ready."

"Don't." She shook her head. "I know the risks."

"Risks? This is madness. We don't even know what that spell does. Is it a weapon? Something that can kill Headwaters? We don't know. And if it isn't? Then how many more spells are we going to have to go through to find one that will work? We turned a dozen pages today and were attacked and nearly blinded. There are hundreds of pages in the book. You can't think we can get through them and somehow miraculously master a spell that will kill Headwaters in the next few hours."

"I think," she said, her voice cold and shaking with anger. "That one of us damn well better find out. You can just stay out here afraid, Brogan. Card, you come with me."

She turned and strode out of the room, Card following behind.

CHAPTER FIFTEEN

Pamela sat and looked busy reading her screen. Abbi crept out from the other room. She touched my hand, then jogged down the hall to catch up with Card and Lula.

Me? Anger washed through me in waves and a raging helplessness filled my chest and clogged my throat. I wanted to yell. To tear this world apart. To grab Lula and drag her away from the book, from this place.

From anything that connected us to gods or the Route or magic.

We were not ready to use the god magic in the book.

We were not skilled enough.

Revenge would only get us dead.

It was a trap. Meeting Headwaters on his terms was so clearly a trap. But Lula was set on killing him now, with the book, with unbridled power.

With or without me.

Fuck.

"You don't need my opinion," Pamela said quietly. "But I'm on your side. No one should be messing with magic that strong. If there's something I can do to talk Lula out of it, I'll try."

I huffed a laugh that was more of a choked sob. "You don't know her like I do."

"No, I don't. Is there anything that would change her mind?"

I took a breath, let it out. "No."

And that was the answer then, grim as it was. I couldn't talk her out of this. She had chosen our path, our fate.

She might have thrown my fear in my face (and she was not wrong, the power in the book terrified me), but she'd done it knowing I wouldn't walk away from her, would never leave her behind to face danger without me.

Our lives were permanently entwined.

So, too, I'd always known, were our deaths.

I'd brought the glass of water out with me when I'd heard Lula on the call with Headwaters. I must have set it on the table.

I picked it up now and drank it down.

We only had hours until dawn. So little time to find the spell we needed. Me standing out here angry wasn't going to give us more time, wasn't going to give *me* more time to learn what I needed to learn to kill Headwaters.

"I hope you've got a hearty dinner lined up," I said. "Something we can eat quick."

"Will do. You want to take some water in with you? I've got sealed bottles."

"Yeah, that'd be good."

Pamela left for the kitchen. I closed my eyes. I'd never been a praying man, and the way I knew the gods, I didn't intend to become one.

Still, I cleared my mind and took breaths to calm my racing emotions and thoughts.

It was unfair how little of the last hundred years I'd been able to truly spend with Lu. Fleeting minutes stitched together from the magic pocket watch that could stop time.

Only these last months had I been alive, real, solid and able to touch her. Hold her.

Now Headwaters and the gods and their damned magic were going to take that all away from me again.

"You better let us in this time, Death," I muttered. "Because I am not letting her soul go without me."

The door to the kitchen opened and Pamela handed me a twelve-pack of bottled water.

"Thanks."

"Is there anything I can do?" Her usually happy face was drawn with worry.

"Save me a shot of whisky?"

"You got it. We're scouting the meeting place. Grandpa's already headed there."

"Tell him to be careful."

"He's a hunter. He knows how to stay beneath the radar. Luck Brogan. If anyone on this Earth can tame the book, it's you and Lula."

"We'll find out, or die trying, I suppose." I gave her a nod and walked down the hall to the safe room.

The door was shut, but Abbi stood outside it.

"I'm sorry," she said, her eyes filling with tears. "I'm sorry Headwaters made you do this. Do you think I can make Lula go to sleep for long enough she'll forget all about it?"

"I think you could do that. But I think she would know you'd done it, and be very, very angry at you. We don't use magic on the people we love."

"Not even to help them stay alive?"

"Not when they've made their decision. It's her life, Abbi. It's mine too. I gave her my soul years ago and it's still hers, just as her soul is mine. If she's walking this path, I'm walking it too."

"Maybe I'll put you both to sleep," she grumbled.

I touched her shoulder. "Give us a little hope instead, okay? We've pulled off the impossible before."

"When?"

"When I convinced you to eat a vegetable instead of a cookie."

"That was a trick!" she said. "I thought a sugar pea was a cookie. I liked it, though."

I smiled. She lunged and hugged me.

I hugged her back. "Hey, now. We don't know how this is going to work out. Let's not give up before we begin."

She nodded, then pulled away. "I told them you would come."

"You were right. Of course."

"Of course."

I reached over and gingerly rested my hand on the latch. No magic sparked, so I opened the door and walked in, Abbi right behind me.

Lu stood with her arms crossed over her chest, facing Card who was talking in quiet tones. She didn't look happy with what he was saying but wasn't arguing.

Her gaze cut to me, golden eyes liquid light in the shadow of the room. I knew she'd heard what I'd said to Abbi. Maybe even what I'd said to Pamela. Her cheeks heated, a rare blush washing across her face, but she tipped her chin up.

Card looked over his shoulder, and his expression was a mix of regret and acceptance.

"Okay. Now we can go forward," he said. "It takes both of you. As I was saying to Lula, there are no short-cuts. Not with this book. It isn't a magic that can be controlled. It can only be used the way it wants to be used, and it wants the both of you to use it. Not one or the other."

"I'm going to step out so you two can talk. Call me back in if you want to go forward with the book."

He walked out, taking Abbi with him, not that it would matter much. She had big ears. She'd hear everything we said.

"You're here," Lu said.

"You know I'd never leave you behind. Where you go, Lula Gauge, I go."

She wiped the tear tracking her cheek with the back of her hand. "I'm angry," she said. "But I'm not angry at you."

"Fair," I said. "I'm angry too. Not at you."

I crossed the room to stand in front of her. I opened my arms. "Too angry for me to hold you?"

She shook her head. "No. Never." She leaned into

me, her arms unlocking and wrapping around my hips. Her palms, pressed against my back, radiated heat.

I kept my breathing even and slow, and after a moment or two, her breathing settled, calmed, matching mine.

"I know I'm wrong," she said. "I know we're not ready to use the book. But Headwaters has never stuck his head out—not in a hundred years. I've never known where he was, or what he was. And I've been dealing with him for decades."

"Through a third party," I said. "A monster like that has his own ways to throw hunters off his trail. You can't blame yourself for not knowing."

"That's only part of it," she said. "We're running out of time."

She leaned back to look at me. "I can feel it, can't you? More and more gods are looking for us, looking for the book. More and more people are getting involved with us trying to use the book, or hide the book, or destroy the book."

"Pretty sure destruction isn't on the table."

"I know. But if it were…"

"That would be my first choice, yes."

"Even if we don't go to meet Headwaters," she said, "even if we just stay here, holed up, trying to find the perfect spell that will kill Headwaters, stop Atë, stop Mithra, and Apep, and all the other gods…how long do you think we'd have before we'd be found?"

The hunters had good wards, the magic here was old, established. We had all their tricks on our side, along with a powerful wizard, the moon rabbit, and Ricky with her resources of the Crossroads.

We had Cupid and Raven on our side too.

But stacking all of that against the unknown, the wrath of three, maybe more gods?

"Not long," I said truthfully. "A week, at the most, before we'd need to find another bolt hole."

"I think so too. So, this is it. This *is* our chance. We find the spell, we use the god magic and cast it at Headwaters with everything we have. No matter the cost. This is it. This is where we were always headed, whether we liked it or not."

"I agree, I *can* agree with all that. I hate it, though. That these are our choices. But at least we still have choices.

"But Lu, there's one thing I don't agree with. The cost matters. Your life matters. If there's a way to use this magic without it killing us, then that's what I want to do. Even if it's harder. Even if it takes us longer."

She hesitated. When my wife made up her mind about something, she did not doubt herself, she did not back down. She had made up her mind that tomorrow was her one and only chance to kill the monster who had destroyed our lives.

I needed her to see that we might have other chances.

"If we find a spell that can kill Headwaters," I said, "I'm all in. If we find one that can trap Headwaters…"

She was already shaking her head.

"…trap Headwaters to give us time to find the spell that will kill him, then I'm all in for that too. You might think we only get one chance at the bastard, but maybe we can hit him more than once. With more than one weapon.

"Can you agree with that?"

"I don't want to agree…I want him dead. But if we can trap him, then kill him, yes."

"Fair and good," I said. "We have a plan B."

"I don't know how you've stayed so optimistic after everything that's happened."

"Did you just call me naive?"

"No. Optimistic. We only get one chance at this, Brogan. The world would never bend to our favor and let us have a plan B."

"We don't need the world to give us favors. We make our own luck. Always have."

"Except for the Blarney Stone!" Abbi yelled through the door. "That was good luck we got with a kiss!"

"She's not wrong," I whispered. "But she is *very* nosy."

"No, I'm not! I can't help it if I can see things. And hear things. I'm so good at it!"

Lu stepped back, her hands dragging down my forearms, to catch my fingers.

"I'm sorry," she said quietly. "I'm sorry, Brogan. I have to do this."

"No apologies. Not to me. I know we're out of time. I want that monster obliterated, so Atë can never use it to turn someone else into what we are—tools for gods to access the book's power."

"Yes," she said. "Abbi. Tell Card he can come back in."

Card entered the room. He had a small brass pocket mirror in his hand that swirled with magic.

"That's new," I said.

"Ricky just found it."

"Is she here?" Lu asked.

"No, the Crossroads found a way to transfer the mirror to the Scout. Scout's a dragon, right? You can tell me."

"Scout is the hunter's business," I said, not wanting to share something they hadn't already shared with him.

"Well, *Scout*, whatever it is, hooked up with the Crossroads, and now I have the mirror."

"What does it do?" Abbi asked.

"It shows me the true intention of god spells."

"The hell," I said. "Are you sure?"

Card flashed me a giddy grin. "Absolutely sure. Not an easy thing to track down. I didn't even know these still existed, but the Crossroads dug it up. Now we can see what those spells can really do."

"How do you use it?" Lu asked.

"Oh, I don't. This goes in the circle with you. Brogan's going to use it."

"And the glasses?" I asked.

"Yes, so I can see what you see and confirm it. We need to arrange a few things. You'll need a table to hold the book and two chairs, if this is going to work the way I think it will."

The door opened (did everyone in the place have a key to it now?), and Abbi came through with a wooden chair.

"I needed some help," she said.

"Hope these are okay." Josie followed Abbi with another wooden chair, and Pamela followed her with a small end table. "We can scrounge up something else if not."

"That should work," Card said. "Just put them down there, mind the sigils."

They did so. Pamela gave Lula a look then checked my expression.

"We're good," I said. "Keep the whisky at the ready, though."

"That," she said, "I can do. Luck, Gauges. See you on the other side."

She took Josie's hand and they walked out, Card shutting the door behind them. He waved his hands to activate the warding spells, then pointed at the chairs.

"Get those in the circle and place them back-to-back," Card said. "Lula, you want the table in front of you."

This was it, the point of no return.

I glanced at the door, and for a moment, I tried to imagine what my life would be like if I had made different choices. But no images came to me, because this was the only life I wanted. The one with Lula at my side.

I picked up the chair and stepped into the circle of spells.

CHAPTER SIXTEEN

"Got it?" Card asked.

"We've gone over it half a dozen times," I said. "If I don't have it by now, not sure you asking again is gonna change anything."

Lula and I sat on the chairs inside the sigil circle, our backs to each other. She had the book propped on the table in front of her. I was wearing the magic glasses and holding the scrying mirror in my hand above my shoulder.

I angled the mirror so I could see the book in its reflection.

"Then begin," Card said.

"I'm ready when you are, love."

Lu inhaled, exhaled, and opened the book. It was the same spell we'd last seen, the one that seemed to be nothing but plain ink on the page.

But this time the words made sense. More than that, the *intent* of the words was clear, like a diagram had been drawn behind the words to show what the spell should be used for.

Card whistled.

"Transformation?" I guessed.

"Yes!" Card said. "Oh, the mirror is brilliant. Okay, can you see the power? It's subtle, it's going to be subtle. You might sense it as a smell or a taste or a sound."

"Black pepper."

"That's it. Focus on that. I can't see lines of power connected to it. I still think this is a lost god spell. Let's see if it has any juice."

"You want me to transform something?"

"I want you to cast the spell to transform something."

"Something small," Lu suggested.

"The pillow?" Abbi picked up a pillow off the cot where she was sitting.

"How about a bottle of water?" Card said.

Abbi put the pillow down and retrieved the water instead. "Do I take it to them?"

"Brogan needs to step out for it," Card said.

I dutifully followed orders, then returned to sit with the mirror in one hand and the bottle in the other.

"How?" I asked.

"Hold in your mind's eye exactly what you want the bottle to transform into," Card said. "Then you need to speak the words. All of them. You don't have to do it quickly, but you have to get through from the start to the finish. Take your time. All through in one."

"I don't speak that language, what if I say it wrong?"

"You won't. Lu," he said, "the book might be hard to keep still while he's casting."

"I know," she said.

I rolled the water bottle in my hand and let my thoughts wander for a moment. I wanted to transform it into something harmless. Something I could keep focused on, something I wouldn't forget no matter what happened during the spell.

There would be a price to pay for this, I assumed. Nothing the gods gave came without strings attached. And those strings were likely to strangle.

Something small. Something beautiful. Harmless.

Something that would make Lula smile.

"Ready," I said.

"All through in one," Card repeated.

I held the vision in my mind and began reciting the words.

They were strange in my mouth, musical in a way I'd never experienced, but with hard stops that had me gasping for breath before continuing on.

I held tight to the mirror and didn't dare look away. Black pepper filled my mouth, my nose, my lungs. My eyes watered, my throat was on fire, but I spoke every syllable to the last.

The earth shook, then one hard thump echoed as if a boulder had rolled down a mountain and struck a brick wall.

The spell lifted, the air smelled of cool breezes and mint.

I coughed into my arm, hacking up the aftertaste of power. Everything in me felt raw.

"Oh, well done," Card said. "Brogan, Lula. How are you?"

"I'm okay," Lula said. "Brogan?"

"Fine." It came out thin, like I'd been shouting for days.

Or breathing god power.

"Can I close the book? Did it work?" Lula asked

"Close the book," Card said. "Brogan?"

Lula shut the cover, and I lowered the mirror in my shaking hand.

We still sat in the chairs, back-to- back. The room was still the room. Abbi and Card were still whole. And whatever the boulder collision had been, it seemed to be gone now.

But there was something in my hand that hadn't been there just a moment before.

I stood, my knees stiff, legs feeling like they were covered in cement. I walked around to Lula. "It worked."

Her eyes went wide.

In my hand, I held a small bundle of wild asters. The flowers were purple with yellow centers, gold shining along the edge of each petal.

"You turned it into wildflowers?" she asked.

"I turned it into something beautiful. Something that reminds me of you." I gave them to her, and she drew them to face to smell the sweet perfume.

"It feels like flowers," she said. "It smells like honey-suckle. Asters don't smell like honeysuckle."

"I like honeysuckle," I said. "It reminds me of summer, of us."

"Transformation," Card said. "The spell followed what Brogan had in his mind. It won't ever be a water bottle again. Well, unless you want to cast that spell to change it back."

"No," I said, clearing my throat. "Once is enough to prove we can use the lost god spell. That we can use the book."

"I thought all the spells in the book were big and mean," Abbi said.

Card made a sound. "None of us can know what the gods were thinking when they put this book together."

"Raven said they made it on a whim," I said. "And promptly forgot about it."

"Which means for some of the gods," Card said, "it wasn't important or consequential. So, there might be more spells that won't automatically destroy."

"Transformation can be used for evil in the wrong hands," Lu said. She smelled the asters again. "Or for something simple and beautiful."

She offered me the flowers, but I shook my head. "They're for you."

She smiled and tucked them into her braid. "I love you."

I cupped her face. "I love you."

I started coughing and turned my head into my shoulder until the bout passed.

Lu left the circle and took a bottle of water from Abbi. She motioned me out of the protective circle and gave it to me. "Drink."

I did and it helped soothe my raw throat. I handed

the empty bottle out for Abbi to take away, then sat back in the chair.

"Ready to look through the book for a spell that will do more than transform a water bottle into a wild-flower?" Card asked.

We entered the circle again and took our seats. I lifted the mirror. "Ready."

Lu took a breath. "I'm turning the page."

It took hours.

Each spell needed time to resolve into something I could read, and more time for Card and I to agree on what its purpose might be. Some blasted lightning into the room. Some rattled reality or manifested in star-strewn winds.

But we needed the lost god spells, and Lu couldn't just thumb through the book to find pages which appeared to be written in plain ink.

The book wouldn't allow it.

She had to turn each page, wait to see if the spell crackled with magic, or plain ink.

We found two lost god spells. One seemed to summon black holes, the other turned oxygen into diamonds.

We weren't foolish enough to cast either of them.

"You two want to take a break?" Card asked, rubbing his eyes and yawning. "Get some food. Coffee?"

"Yes," I said. "Both."

"One more page," Lula said.

"Love, it's been hours. We'll take a break and get back at it. Half an hour, tops."

"No, I think…" She made a frustrated sound. "I

think one more page. The book seems to want…I think we need to turn one more page before we take a break."

I swore but pushed the glasses back on my face. "One more. But then I need a break, a real break. Deal?"

"Yes. I know. Yes."

"Ready," I said.

"Ready," Card said.

"I'm turning the page," she said.

This spell flared blue, then spidery writing filled the page. It looked like plain ink, although it had a nimbus glow to it.

"Lost god," Card said. "I think it is. Brogan?"

"I think so too." I adjusted the mirror waiting for the words to resolve into something I could read, or a diagram to appear, or some other clue that would tell me what this was.

A chill ran down my spine.

"What?" Lula asked, sensing the change in me.

"It's…dark. I can't see exactly what it does, but it's violent. Card?"

He'd shifted to the edge of his chair. "Agreed. This was meant to destroy."

"How?" Lu asked. "Is it a sword, a bomb, a storm? That stupid diamond thing again?"

"It's a beast," I said, swallowing down the sense of power, of fire kindling through the spider web ink. "Something caged that can be awakened."

None of us said anything.

The mix of relief and horror was uncomfortable. We'd found something that might be powerful enough to kill Headwaters. But if we used this spell, if we released a beast like this upon our enemy, there was no guarantee we'd be able to control what it destroyed.

"Are you going to do the spell now?" Abbi asked, worried. "Because I don't think you should do the spell now, I really don't think you should."

"Lula, will the book allow you to return to the page without having to go through the rest?" Card asked. "Can you mark your place?"

"I know where it is. I know how the book…accesses it. Yes. I think I can find it again."

"Then we all need a break," Card said. "Food, maybe sleep. It's only a few hours before dawn and we have a big decision to make."

We'd been at this all day and night. No wonder I felt like I'd been dragged behind a truck.

"I'm closing the book," Lu said.

She did, and I stood and rolled my shoulders trying to throw off the dread in my gut.

Finding that spell, the one that might kill Headwaters, made this even more real.

We were going to fight Headwaters—kill him—in just a few hours.

Or we were going to cast a spell that would slip our control the moment we unleashed it and destroy us, our family, the world.

I picked up the witch's box and opened it.

Lula looked even paler than normal, the circles darker under her eyes. She might talk a good game, but she was exhausted.

She placed the book in the witch's box. I set it on the floor, draping the shadow cloth over the whole thing.

We left the circle and the room in silence.

Once out in the hall, the fatigue really kicked in. I wanted to sleep for a hundred years.

"Food." Lu took my hand and guided me down the hall straight into the kitchen.

The kitchen was old school industrial but had a table with bench seating at one side.

That's where Lu deposited me.

"Give me a minute," she said, pulling down a cast iron skillet and drawing over a loaf of bread.

I crossed my arms on the table and rested my head there. I closed my eyes for a second, only a second.

"Brogan," Lula's hand stroked down my back. "Food."

I made a sound and she chuckled.

"Yes. Eat something. You'll feel better."

I reluctantly lifted my head.

She held a plate with a huge sandwich on it and piles of potato and corn.

My stomach growled and I sat up.

She settled the food in front of me and sat close so she could lean against my side. She'd made herself a steak—venison, rare—and cut small bites to eat.

Card was already eating a bowl of soup, checking his phone, and Abbi was out in the control room, telling whoever was out there what we'd found.

I picked up the sandwich—layers of meat including some of the venison, surrounded by cheese and tomato, onion and lettuce—and dug in.

I'd never eaten a sandwich so quickly. Then I turned on the fried potatoes and corn she'd broiled and seasoned.

As soon as my plate was cleared, I tuned back into the conversation.

"At the rest stop, might be best," Elmer said. "Good vantage points from there."

"Easy for us to get to, means it will be easy for him too," Lula said. "It's so close to the highway."

"Then back in the hills a bit. But it's where I'd park. We have good access to surveillance and a couple bolt holes if things go south."

Pamela and Josie weren't in the kitchen. I hoped they were sleeping.

Elmer looked fresh, like he'd gotten some shut eye after his reconnaissance of the meeting place with Headwaters.

He also looked relaxed and confident, as if facing this kind of monster was an everyday thing.

He was a hunter and not easily spooked. I'm sure he'd taken on all kinds of evil in his days.

"What about escape routes?" Card asked. "If it goes to hell in a handbasket, I want a way out of there. I'm not going to die in the middle of Nowhere, New Mexico."

"Aren't you a cheerful fella?" Elmer asked.

"Yes. Usually. But right now, I want to cover our asses."

"Fair," the older man said. "Like I said, there are bolt holes. With strong enough magics to keep us hid. Not a lot of cover otherwise. The highway will get you out. There's trails off road too, but no real roads or structures, manmade or otherwise."

"Is there a map?" Card asked.

"Sure. We've got video set up on some of it. I'll show you." He and Card left the kitchen. I glanced at the wall clock.

"Three," I said. "Dawn in what, two hours?"

Lu nodded. "It will take us about an hour to get there. You can catch an hour nap."

"I'll stay up." I yawned hugely. "Help plan."

She tipped her head to the side. The braid, which still had the wild asters twined in it, swung across her back.

"What's to plan?" she asked. "You and I show up at the rest stop, or behind it in the hills. Headwaters comes. We kill Headwaters."

"Contingency plan. Plan B. It's not going to go easily or smoothly. It never does. We don't know how to control that spell. We've never cast it."

"We cast one of the lost god spells. We can cast this one."

"No two of those gods are the same. I don't believe it's that easy. Releasing a beast, Lu? That's a hell of a different thing from transforming water bottles into flowers."

She frowned. I knew I wasn't telling her anything she hadn't already thought about.

"You can't back out on this now, Brogan."

"If you're in this fight, I'm in this fight. You don't walk into danger without me at your side. But," I bent my head to catch her gaze, "this might be our end, our death. Headwaters tore out our souls and stitched them back together the way he wanted. He knows how we're made. He knows how to unmake us.

"Maybe using the beast isn't the best way to go."

"What other choices do we have? Summon a black hole, which will swallow Earth? Turn the oxygen into diamonds, which will kill us all? Turn water bottles into flowers? We have Cupid's favor, Raven's help, Abbi, the hunters, and Card. Do you really think we can't win?"

She leaned back too, her body more fluid than mine, tucking one leg up on the bench.

"I'm saying if I could drop a dime and call Death, I'd ask if he was going to escort us over the threshold this time. Just in case. Because I refuse to be half-alive and impossibly apart from you again."

"You want to call Death?" Abbi asked, popping into the room. "I can call Death."

"Sure," I said. "You can call Death."

"He gave me his number. Plus, it's online. He has a web page!"

"Oh for…" I didn't believe her. Was too tired to think it through, was too tired to be arguing with Lula on a subject I would never win.

"Fine," I said. "Call Death and ask him if we die, if he'll take us together or not at all. I handed her my mobile phone, which I hardly ever used.

Abbi took it and pressed the keypad, then held it to her ear.

CHAPTER SEVENTEEN

"It's ringing!" Abbi said, excited. "Hello? Death?" She paused, waiting for an answer.

I shifted on the bench, suddenly more awake. She really was calling Death. On my phone.

"Oh," she said. "Boo. It's a voice mail. Okay, wait... Hi! Hi, Than. It's Abbi moon rabbit, and Brogan and Lula, oh, they're Brogan and Lula Gauge, I think you met them? You gave Brogan a kite? A dream kite?

"They want to know if you will let them die if Headwaters kills them because they don't want to be apart and sad and lonely. Okay. Thank you. We're gonna go kill stuff now. Bye!"

She ended the call. "There. Do you think he'll call back?"

I took my phone and shook my head, life having fully jumped the rails, and me too tired to make sense of it. "No, Pumpkin, I don't suppose."

"Well, maybe." She shrugged. "Are we going to bed now?"

"Not much time left," I noted.

"Enough not to spend it arguing or worrying." Lula stood and took my hand. "Let's get you some shut eye."

I rose with her, and Abbi took my other hand. "Can I come too?"

"Of course," I tugged her toward the door, encouraging her through it in front of us.

The three of us climbed into bed in the room with the stars overhead, me on the outside, Lula in my arms, and Abbi hugging her. We hadn't changed out of our clothes, though we'd shed our boots. Lorde had followed along and jumped up to lay herself across our feet.

"I'm not going to sleep," I said. "But if I do, wake me up."

"Mmmm," Lula said.

If she said any more, I didn't hear her.

THE DRIVE WENT by faster than I expected. Lu, me, and Abbi (who had fiercely refused to stay behind) rode in the truck. The spell book of the gods was wrapped in the shadow cloth, shut away in the witch's box.

We'd left Lorde behind with plenty of water and food and a place where she could go to the bathroom. She hadn't been happy about it, but Lu and I had agreed we couldn't risk her getting hurt.

Though we'd made Lorde stay behind, we'd been unsuccessful in talking the hunters and Cardamom into doing the same.

None of them had a weapon that could kill Head-waters. Only Lula and I could cast the spells in the book.

But the Walches knew the land like the backs of their hands, and Cardamom insisted his magic could cloak and help defend us.

Abbi, of course, had her mortar and pestle.

I'd tucked the scrying mirror in my pocket.

"We're almost there," Lu said.

I rubbed my hand over my mouth and nodded. I was just as hungry for Headwaters' death as Lu, and had finally admitted it could take us several more lifetimes to get good enough to control the spell, to control the beast within it.

We didn't have those several lifetimes.

Lu slowed and signaled the turn to the rest stop.

A wooden sign with CONTINENTAL DIVIDE arching across it indicated this was the exact point where the continental United States essentially broke in two, weather from one side rising against the western edge of the mountains, and weather from the east side crashing from the other.

The rest stop wasn't much—a paved parking area on a rise above the highway which intersected the Divide, a few placards explaining what the Divide was, and a restroom. But the view of the land was stunning.

Hills rose around us. Even though it was still dark, it was clear, the sky just the smallest bit lighter than the hills.

Lu parked the truck, and the hunters rolled up beside us.

Elmer lowered his window. I did the same. "We're

gonna tuck the car back there behind the scrub," he said. "Then we'll take off on foot. Don't look for us. We'll be watching. We'll be there when you need us."

"Safe travels," I said.

The plan hadn't gotten more complicated. We were here before dawn, enough time for the Walches to spread out and man the bolt holes that might be our only escape route out.

They'd activated cameras and magical items which could survey a wide area and would rely on those to find us if the battle with Headwaters went wrong.

It was obviously going to go wrong.

The Walches piled out of their car and headed off.

Cardamon walked over to us. "I'm coming with you. I'll be out of line of sight, but I want to know exactly where you make your stand.

"Not sure why you're telling us," I said. "It's not like we can argue any of you out of this insane plan."

"Exactly." His smile was bright in the darkness. "I've faced down power, enormous power. Didn't always come out of those fights whole. But I'm still alive."

"Your point?" I pushed the door and got out. Abbi bounced down after me, kitten Hado on her heels.

I moved around to the back for the witch's box.

"You're still alive too."

Lula's door opened with a creak, then clunked shut.

Card touched my arm. "Don't forget things can change in a flash. Fate can tip her hand."

"If Fate was ever on our side," I said, "she'd have tipped her hand by now."

"We don't know the minds of gods."

"Not that it would make any difference."

Lu strode over to us her boots scraping gravel over pavement.

"This way," she said.

This was it. No more time to argue or speculate. Before Headwaters arrived, we needed to find the ground where we would make our stand.

Lu moved swiftly and silently across the lot and located an animal trail we followed into the hills.

I walked behind her, Abbi behind me, Card taking up the rear.

None of us spoke, saving our breath for the hike, keeping our ears and eyes open for any sign of Headwaters arriving early.

My stomach rolled with nerves and anger, but I pushed panic, fear, worry, and rage away.

If we were going to get through this, one of us needed to keep a level head.

That one of us was me.

I focused on my feet, on the smell of damp and dust, on the coolness of the air in my lungs.

We had walked this world for decades, traveled the Route over and over. Images of the good times flashed through my mind—those stolen moments together in graveyards, magic watch stopping time long enough for us to touch. Lu's birthday just a few weeks ago, her surprise and delight at the cake and gifts.

Nights in the back of the truck with the stars above us, when all the world breathed, and we breathed with it.

It hadn't been enough. But then a million lifetimes wouldn't be enough with Lula.

Lu took turns that led us farther and farther from the highway.

The hum and rush of cars and trucks faded into nothing. Only the sound of our footsteps broke the stillness of the early morning.

Not even the birds made noise.

"Here," Lu said. She stopped on a rise with higher hills behind us to the north. "I think here."

It was a good choice. We had a clear view for several miles, the ground spreading out in the distance to the west, south, and east. We'd be able to see Headwaters' approach.

We'd have space to cast the spell that contained the beast. We'd have space to fight.

The sky was bruised gray and warm taupe, a flat, cloudless pre-dawn promising heat.

"Good." Card strode off, quickly touching the scrub around us, whispering his magic to the plants, the stones, the soil.

Half-dryad meant he had a lot of sway with the magic and powers of the living world, growing things. I figured we could use their help too.

"I hear him," Abbi said.

"Headwaters?"

She nodded. "He's getting closer."

"Which direction?" Lu asked.

Abbi pointed south.

Lula's gaze searched for me, and I nodded.

"Let's set up."

I put the witch's box on the ground and pulled the mirror out of my pocket. I removed the shadow cloth and opened the lid.

Lula knelt and lifted the book out of the box.

Abbi darted behind us, looking for cover. She crouched in the shadow of a boulder, Hado helping her fade even more into the dim corners of the morning.

"No talking," I said.

"No talking," Lu agreed. "No negotiations, no threats."

"No negotiations, no threats," I said. "As soon as we know it's him, we unleash the spell."

"Yes."

"Card?" I asked. But even as the light spread like soft static through the darkness, I realized Card was gone, hidden.

Lu stood, and I stood beside her. We had practiced this—how she would hold the book so I could stand with my back to hers, the mirror positioned so I could see the page to cast the spell.

I didn't want to take that position yet, though. Not until I saw Headwaters with my own eyes.

It felt like time belly-crawled through wet sand, an endless grinding pace.

It was cold enough, I wished I'd worn a hat, but still, sweat gathered at my hairline.

The wind picked up, and the eastern sky bloomed yellow, orange, rose, fading up to soft blue.

Moments later, the sun rose.

"He's here," Abbi whispered into the brutal silence.

Lu lifted her chin and squared her shoulders. I followed her gaze.

Headwaters strolled our way. To say he was human was like comparing a theater mask to a living actor's face.

He was tall, easily eight feet, and swathed in layers of wool and satin and leather that gave him a patchwork opulence.

His hands were gloved, his face obscured by a heavy hood.

Nightmares were sketched in his shadow, horrors crawled between his feet.

It had been a hundred years since I'd seen this monster, and in those years he had become more fetid, his body twisted with rot, swollen with disease.

He saw us, too, and paused six yards distant.

"Brogan Gauge," it purred, voice low and sonorous. "I see your flesh, I see your bones, I see your soul. Such sweet fear in you. Show me how alive you are."

A sharp pain flared in my chest, like a fist squeezing my heart. My knees went soft, but I refused to fall, to kneel. I grunted and panted through the pain.

"Lula Gauge," he sang. "How beautiful you have become."

She jerked her head as if she'd been slapped and stumbled backward. Bruises spread across her neck and up her cheeks.

She glanced at me, eyes wide and panicked.

Then I did the hardest thing I'd ever done in my life —I turned my back on the monster.

Lu opened the book.

"You touch it," the monster gasped, "the spell book."

I tipped the mirror, trying to steady my hand to catch the words in the glass. I filled my lungs and opened my mouth.

The spell was fire across my tongue, down my throat, in my belly. Sounds collided, blended, broke apart, skittering painfully between my teeth.

This wasn't like the transformation spell. There would be no beautiful flowers at the end of it.

This spell was violence and pain, it was horror. Each word tore out of my chest and left me raw.

Lu's hands shook, and still I spoke.

The mirror cracked, and still I spoke.

Thunder growled across the sky, lightning bombarding the horizon. The wind howled across the plain, kicking dirt and debris as the ground rumbled.

Still, I spoke.

I couldn't see Headwaters, didn't dare look away from the mirror, from the spell.

I wouldn't see his attack when it came.

My heartbeat went ragged, making it hard to pull in enough breath fast enough to continue the spell.

All through in one, Card's words came back to me.

I had to finish the spell, or none of this would work.

Lu's entire body shook. I had to constantly adjust the mirror to keep the spell in view.

Then the last word ripped out of my lungs, and everything went suddenly, painfully silent.

Nothing happened.

The spell didn't do anything.

I spun forward, every muscle throbbing. I was absolutely horse-whipped. It took everything I had not to drop the mirror.

Headwaters' hood was thrown back revealing a face of horror that had been permanently etched in my brain.

He was vampire, only by the paleness of his skin and the hook of fangs over thin, blood red lips. His forehead was wide and protruded over cat-like eyes the color of wet ash. Yellow hair slicked his skull and hung lank to his shoulders.

If he had ever been human, there was no sign of it now, his expression alien and intense and utterly devoid of soul.

He raised his hand—

—just as the spell exploded.

I crashed to the ground, Lula next to me, pinned like a giant foot was crushing us.

I couldn't breathe.

The air was gone—

—*diamonds? I wondered, deliriously. Had we cast the wrong spell?*—

—the sky and earth melted into mind-twisting terrors I could not describe.

I couldn't feel my body, but still, I reached for Lula.

I couldn't feel her hand, but I knew it was in mine.

The world exploded again and a great howling filled the air.

Something huge loomed above us, so large it blocked out the sun.

It had eyes—too many.

It had limbs—too many.

Its teeth were massive and stained with blood. Its body was built of fur and bone and scales.

The beast.

It howled, but it did not attack us.

It did not attack Headwaters.

It swung its head to the sky and exploded into smoke.

The sun burned again, the ground solid beneath me, the sky blue and arching overhead.

I sucked air, like I'd just dug up out of my own grave, and tasted blood and ash.

Lu's hand in mine was warm.

All the rest of me was frozen.

The book was closed in Lu's arms.

The beast was gone. It had broken free from the book and disappeared.

We had failed.

"You are nothing," Headwaters spat. "How dare you call on god magic. How dare you disobey me."

I rolled onto my side, hands and knees, my head hanging. The world was blacking out and snapping back into place. Bright, much too bright.

I pushed upward because Lula was moving, on her knees, then struggling to her feet.

We weren't going to die on our knees.

"We obey no god," I said, "or the worthless castoffs they create."

Headwaters laughed, and it was rotted and cruel.

"You think you can stand against me? I *made* you what you are. I control your souls."

Lula could barely lift the book, but she drew it up to her chest and opened it.

The spells were all we had.

It would kill us, but we were going to cast god magic again.

"No." Headwaters didn't yell, didn't even raise his voice. But it sounded like a mountain falling, that one word hammering painfully through my brain.

Lula staggered and almost fell.

"I tore your souls apart once," he hissed. "I forced the bloody pieces to join and twist and scar. I can rip them from your bodies and end you for good."

He raised his hand again and my back bowed like I was caught on meat hooks.

I screamed.

Movement to my left shifted, something fast I couldn't track.

Abbi stood in front of us.

Not in the guise of a child, but someone, some*thing* older and more powerful. Her mortar glowed in her hands, the pestle carved from stars, a cloak of shadow rising like wings behind her.

I tried to call out for her. To tell her to run.

She was a deity.

She was powerful.

But Headwaters was powerful too.

Abbi threw magic at the monster.

Headwaters lunged, inhumanly fast, his claws extended, aimed at her throat.

A fissure of light cracked open in the space right behind Abbi.

Cardamom stepped through a portal, whipping fireball after fireball of magic at Headwaters.

But not even a powerful wizard could stop that monstrosity.

I reached for Abbi…

…and time stopped.

Headwaters was frozen mid-leap, Cardamom's magic wrapped around his throat, Abbi's magic shrouding his head.

Abbi and Card were frozen too.

Card's fingertips rested on Abbi's shoulder, ready to pull her back through the portal in space he had opened.

Everything in the world was frozen.

Except Lula and me.

Dried blood tracked like tears from the corners of her eyes, catching her braid which had swung forward. The wildflowers we'd created with lost god power were still tucked in her braid, blood blackening the petals.

But in her hand was the magic pocket watch that could stop time, her thumb pressing the stem.

Clever, clever woman.

We only had a minute, had never been able to endure the stoppage of time any longer than that.

"We have to save Abbi," I said. "We have to run."

Lula smiled, but there were tears in her eyes. Her hand shook. "You aren't strong enough to run. You aren't fast enough. Neither am I."

She was right.

I was exhausted to the point my vision was blurring. I couldn't run.

For her to admit she couldn't either, meant she was just as depleted as I was.

I lifted my hand and put it over hers, helping her keep time paused.

"I love you, Lula Gauge," I said as I would always say.

"I love you, Brogan Gauge," she said.

It was our hello. It was our pledge across too many lonely years.

And now, it was our good-bye.

"We're here to kill the bastard," I said, shifting our hold so it was my thumb on the watch stem instead of hers. "Pick up that damn book."

CHAPTER EIGHTEEN

A minute can spin out in a flash, or it can contain infinities.

But however much time this minute contained, it was all we had left to finally have our revenge.

Lu picked up the book. She didn't seem to notice her hands were blistered and burned. She opened the cover.

The page was a lost god spell. Not the violent one that had released the beast. It was the first one we'd cast to transform a simple bottle of water into wildflowers.

I didn't know if we could cast the spell again.

But I knew exactly how I wanted to use it now.

I didn't need the mirror. The spell had written itself into me, every syllable, every word, burned and permanent.

I just had to say each word within the seconds we had left.

All through in one.

I focused on the watch in my hand, on its magic that stopped time.

I drew upon the lost god's magic to transform it.

Lula trembled beside me. I shook as the world went frigid.

Each word was harder to speak, each utterance softer, my voice raw and used until it was nothing, barely a whisper, a gasp, a breath.

All through in one.

Before the last word, Lu grabbed my hand that held the watch.

Except it wasn't a watch. Not anymore.

It was our hatred, our anger.

It was a pulsing glob of magic and time, a bomb built for one purpose—to snuff out the spark of life in the horrifying creature who had destroyed our souls.

To kill a powerful thing created by a powerful god.

But I did not say the final word. Could not say it until the weapon was buried in that monster's chest.

Lu knew it. Somehow she knew. She took a step, forcing me forward with her. I couldn't feel my legs, didn't know if I lifted my feet or if Lu dragged me there.

She stopped, panting through clenched teeth, and her gaze met mine.

I nodded.

She yelled and thrust my hand upward with enough force that we punched through the monster's flesh and bone.

My thumb slipped off the watch stem.

I screamed the last word of the spell with everything left in me.

Time snapped back into motion—

—Abbi yelled—

—Cardamom yanked her through the portal—

—Lula laughed as a hundred lightning bolts struck the ground, caging us and the monster in electric fire—

—this was our death. But gods be damned, we were taking that fucking monster out with us.

An inferno of black flames engulfed Headwaters, devouring flesh, bone, and blood.

He twisted and convulsed, scrabbling at his flesh to get away from the agony.

Before Headwaters hit the ground, he evaporated, molecules, atoms, nothing.

Then time itself exploded.

SHE WAS WALKING down the street and suddenly, I couldn't breathe. I'd been working since dawn the day before, breaking rock, digging ditches for the farm just east of town. The farmer had sent me on my way with barely a penny in my pocket.

So I was in town, cleaned up as best I could in the stream, and looking for work.

But seeing her stopped me in my tracks.

She turned to look at me, her hair soft autumn fire, her eyes a hazel more gold than green.

She smiled, and I knew my heart would never be my own again.

THE NIGHT WAS BITTERLY COLD, snow up to my knees. But still I kept walking. Lula was waiting for me, said she'd have a cup of coffee ready, even if I got to the bakery after closing hours.

By the time I got there, it was nearing midnight.

I almost turned away.

But I knocked with frozen fingers.

Lula opened the door, a heavy shawl over her shoulders, and ushered me in.

She brewed us both a cup of coffee, but her smile warmed me more than the welcome heat from the Franklin stove.

I KISSED HER, a trembling brush of lips asking questions I could not speak.

SHE KISSED ME BACK.

WE DANCED. She laughed at my clumsiness, my feet in the wrong places, on the wrong beat, as the band sawed out a summer tune.

THEY WOULD BE our wedding vows, and we'd say them soon, so soon, beneath the big tree, just her and I and the pastor.

I repeated mine every night like a ritual as I waited to marry the woman I loved.

I LAY DYING, watching the monster feed on her.

Our gazes had locked and then…

…then everything had gone black. It was a good blackness. Peaceful, warm.

Until I'd woken into the shattering of her scream.

She: bent over my unbreathing, unresponsive body.

Me: standing above myself—poor dead bastard—unable to close the deal, finish the story.

There was no white light guiding me up, no red flames dragging me down. I wouldn't have wanted them anyway. All I wanted was her.

THE MONSTER EVAPORATED and time shattered, hammering me, us, reality, into a million pieces that could never be glued back together.

Still, I reached for her, for any shred of her I could hold, protect, love…and she reached for me…

"THE ANSWER," a low, droll voice I'd heard somewhere, somewhen before said, "is still no, Brogan Gauge. I am, as I have said before, rather occupied with my vacation. You may remind the moon rabbit of such."

Another voice, much warmer, with power that glowed gold with leaden shadows, said, "You are mine still. This will not be your end."

Darkness and light, time and stasis, life and death, reality and destruction flickered.

I breathed again, lived again.

I was sitting in our old silver truck, on the twisted road near the hunter's hideout, Lula—beautiful, living, breathing Lula—next to me. The book was in her lap, the blisters on her hands already healed.

I should be rattled, shocked, reeling from the whiplash of life and almost death. But my head was clear, my heartbeat steady.

Cupid stood outside the truck, his god power so bright, I winced. He was swathed in golden armor, massive pure white wings spread out behind him, a huge bow and brutal arrows in his hands.

"Apep knows where you are," he said. "He knows you have the book. Casting the spell—both of them—gave you away. You need to run. Now. Back to the hideout. Back to the hunters."

He snapped his fingers and the truck engine growled.

The wind buffeted us, rocking the truck.

"Run!" Cupid took three great strides and the sky thundered as he disappeared.

"Lu are you? Are we?" I said.

She nodded. "The box. Open the box."

I spotted the witch's box by my feet and hurriedly pulled off the shadow cloth and lid.

She dropped the book inside.

I covered the box, and Lula gunned the engine, tearing down the rutted trail at speed.

I slid over the bench seat and wrapped my arm around her.

"Abbi?" Lula asked, as we jerked and jostled down the rough trail.

"Card got her," I said, searching through my jumbled, scattered memories. "I think he saved her with magic."

"The Walches?"

"I don't know."

The sky was dark, the sun swallowed whole by heavy black clouds crackling with silver-shot lightning.

That wasn't a natural storm building above us. That was god power clawing across the heavens.

"How did we? Who?" she asked.

"Death," I said. "Cupid. How far?"

Lula shook her head. "Miles. Ten?"

Ten wasn't good. Ten was a lot when there was a god on your heels.

The sky caught fire—literal red flames licking across the bellies of the clouds, burning and churning.

A massive serpent—at least a mile long and made of smoke and fire and onyx—slithered out of the sky.

The snake blasted into the land behind us, shaking the world. Its head was the size of a mountain, its scales gold and ivory with onyx bands. It opened its jaw and its fangs dripped with venom.

Apep, the god of chaos.

Lu snarled and glanced in the side view mirror. "Brogan?"

"Give me your daggers." I couldn't hold the book to

cast a spell. Lula couldn't stop driving. The watch was gone. Her daggers and my knife were the last weapons we had.

"That won't be enough—" she started to say. "Look!"

I twisted in the seat, peering behind us.

A tornado of crows, thousands, millions, surrounded the snake, the noise loud enough to drown out the thunder.

When the crows lifted, crying to the sky, the snake was gone.

"Raven," I said.

I turned back around, just as the giant snake punched up out of the sandy soil in front of us.

"Lu!"

She cranked the wheel, and the truck skittered and fish tailed.

The huge snake sideswiped the truck—

—just as a massive arrow pierced its eye, pinning its head to the ground.

Cupid, thirty feet tall, strode into the fray, shooting arrow after arrow into the snake's flesh.

The snake writhed free of the arrows and struck.

Cupid winged upward, narrowly avoiding the hit. He drew a massive sword and dove down, ramming the blade into the snake's head.

The sky bellowed in a cacophony of pain.

The gods disappeared.

Lu kept her foot on the gas. "What do you see? Are they out there?"

"Gone." I bent to scan the sky through the windows. "I can't see them. Storm's coming on strong, coming our way. Sky's on fire."

"We can't," Lu said. "We can't go to the hunters. We'd bring this right to their doorstep."

"If Cupid and Apep are fighting, they won't see where we go."

"They'll always see, Brogan," she said. "The gods always see."

The dials in the dash swung wildly. The truck was slowing. The engine died.

"Lu?"

"Not me."

"Gas?" I asked, my hand on the door latch.

"No."

"Battery?"

"I don't—" She turned the key and nothing happened. "I don't think so."

"I'll look." I opened the door.

"Wait!" Lu snagged my sleeve and held on. "Look." She pointed ahead of us.

Calmly walking our way was Mithra, the god of contracts.

He stopped in front of the truck. "You have run far enough, broken souls. Your road ends here. Cupid cannot save you. Raven cannot save you. The others are all dead."

His words twisted in my heart but I knew it had to be a lie. The others were still alive. Had to be alive.

"Give me the book, pledge fealty to me as your one

and only god, and I will grant you mercy. The book." Mithra snapped his fingers.

A hand wrapped around my throat and jerked me out of the truck. Lula was beside me, both of us in front of the truck, the dead engine radiating heat behind us.

On the ground in front of us was the witch's box.

"Open it," Mithra commanded. "You. He pointed at Lula.

She stiffened and bent. Her braid with the wild asters woven into it swung in front of her as she drooped like a marionette being dragged by its strings.

Her hands were not her own, not under her own power. I could tell by how clumsily she fumbled with the box, how she fought opening the lid, how they went to rigor when she grasped the book.

She pulled it free and stood.

"Good girl," Mithra said. "Now, you, on your knees."

He pointed at me.

I dropped so hard my teeth clacked together. I tasted blood.

"You do not have to sign a contract for me to bind you to me, for me to control you. It is only by my grace that I have allowed you free will all these years. But now, I tire of waiting. You, and the book, are mine."

Lu, somehow, amazingly, had the strength to open the book.

There was one spell, only one that was written in me I could call upon. I opened my mouth, knowing I didn't have the breath, didn't have the strength to cast a third god spell in so short a time.

Not that it would stop me from trying.

"Wild asters?" the odd voice said from behind me. "Of all the choices, you created wild asters?"

Mithra's face lost all color, and his eyes went large. Panic flashed across his face.

"Lost god," he breathed.

CHAPTER NINETEEN

The sky was still on fire. I could see the reflection of red and shadow swirling across the ground.

The wind fluxed hot, then cold, and a spatter of rain rattled briefly like bullets peppering the dust.

It didn't feel like time had stopped—I knew all too well what that was like. But there was a stillness to the world, an *otherness* that sent ice through my veins.

"What are you?" The voice behind us moved forward.

Lula was on my left, and the voice, the lost god, appeared next to her.

Gods could wear any form they wanted. I knew that. But this was a thing I had never seen in my life.

Its head was an ivory mask, rounded at the chin and rising into two points at the top, which floated above a body formed of light, stone, scales, ink. Its arms and legs didn't seem attached but moved fluidly, changing from bone to wing to tentacle to claw.

In the seams and cracks of it was a blackness so deep, it was like staring into the void of space.

"I am the god, Mithra," Mithra answered. "And you are not welcome in this reality, lost god. Leave. Now."

"You mean nothing to me," the lost god mused. "I am that which existed before, I will be that which exists after you have burned to dust."

Mithra laughed. "Return to your hole. This reality refutes you. Nothing holds you here. You are forgotten."

The ivory mask tipped precariously to one side. "I have been remembered, God Mithra. I have been summoned by my spell, locked, and power, latent."

"You have no hold here."

"I do now. These small creatures have gnawed through my chains, chains now consigned to oblivion."

"Those creatures are mine."

"You tire me." There was a huge sound, like an ocean pouring off a cliff.

Mithra threw up his hands as if to ward off an attack.

And disappeared.

I reached for Lula, and she scrabbled backward to me, the book clutched against her chest.

The lost god drifted forward away from us, filling the space Mithra had just occupied.

"Small creatures," the lost god said. "You have called upon my power. You have dared wield my magic." It turned, the mask unreadable.

"Shall I reward you? Or shall I punish you?"

"You will do neither, Ryt." Cupid strode out of the sky. He was still in god form, a warrior in golden armor with huge white wings. "These souls are under my protection."

"Connection, destruction," Ryt said. "You still walk this realm?"

"Longer than you, lost one. There is a war."

"There is always a war."

"You are not a part of this war," Cupid said. "You are not needed here."

The mask tipped as every part of it flowed from one form to another: wind, water, fire, stars.

"The small creatures called me. Stole my fire."

"They cast the spell you wove into the spell book of the gods. As is their right."

Before, I hadn't been able to see eyes in the mask, but now those eyes—large and yellow and alien—focused on me and Lula with painful intensity.

I could not look away, even though it felt like every nerve in my brain was being plucked one by one.

"What are they?" Ryt asked.

A raven winged down from the roiling sky, then Raven, the god, stepped out of its form.

I'd never seen Raven in his god power, not really, not fully. But now, oh, now, he was magnificent.

A warrior, a king, a hunter, a wise man, a fool, black feathers etched with galaxies flowing from his arms and his hair, the light of the sun burning in one hand.

"They are the only thing that will assure your power and magic will never be used without your blessing again," Raven said. "Time has shattered and opened many doors, Ryt. But this path is closed to you. Closed by me."

More movement behind us, then Abbi was at my side, her hand on my shoulder.

Cardamom stood next to Lula, and the hunters were behind him.

They were alive! But they wouldn't be if they stayed here. Not while gods decided if they were going to end reality.

"These souls are under my protection," Cupid said. "Each and all. Go on your way, lost one. Go on your way."

The lost god drifted slowly toward us, disengaged from the Earth, from gravity itself.

Lula's hand reached out for mine. I took it.

We stood, needing to stand when facing a creature of such immense power.

"You chose a flower," Ryt said, the odd voice different now, more curious than before. "Of all the things in the universes, a flower. Why?"

I supposed I could lie but didn't see why I should.

"Love," I said. "I created flowers because I wanted to make Lula smile."

"My power is burned into you now," Ryt said. "Into both of you. My magic. That spell."

"We don't want it," Lula said.

Ryt made a clicking sound. "Shall I remove it, then? Tear it from you? You will explode."

"No." Cupid's voice boomed. "You do not touch them. You do nothing in this realm. It is not for you."

Ryt drifted to a stop in front of Cupid. "I know you, old one. I remember you."

It was a chant, a call demanding a response.

"I know you, old one. I remember you," Cupid replied.

"Are they so valuable? These small creatures. Their pitifully short lives?"

"Yes." The word, the conviction, was heavy as lead, worthy as gold. "Return to your rest, your curiosities, the reality in which you dwell. You are not forgotten."

Cupid didn't waver, his presence solid as the world, the tick of time.

"I do not favor this existence…this old folly…" Ryt grew faint, all of the shifting limbs, body, and mask going transparent, "…but now I will remember it…"

It was a threat. It was a promise.

Then the god was gone.

The sky rumbled, thunder in the distance. A flash of lighting brightened the clouds, then rain, cool cleansing rain, fell.

I shivered, even though I couldn't feel the cold.

"Mithra?" Lu asked. "Apep?"

"Gone," Cupid said. "For now." He was still in golden armor, but was shedding his god power, becoming more human. "I'll make sure they stay that way. Go back with the hunters. Rest. I'll call on you soon."

He took a step and was gone.

"Show off." Raven was just Raven again, wearing a burnt sienna hoodie, jeans, and boots. The only thing different about him was the amulet around his neck that glowed gold like a small sun.

"Let's get out of the weather," he suggested. "Where's that bolt hole of yours?"

"Not sure I want to welcome a god onto my proper-ty," Elmer said. "Especially a trickster god, Raven."

Pamela placed her hand on his arm.

"Do you trust him?" she asked Lula and me.

"Enough," I said.

"Mostly," she said.

"Hey!" Raven said. "We're all friends here. Tell them I'm a friend, Bun Bun."

"I like him," Abbi said. "But sometimes he lies."

"Well, now I'm not going to share my cookies with you."

"You have cookies?"

"I always have cookies. Trickster god, right? Some-times I lie, but sometimes I steal." He waggled his eyebrows and pulled a plate with a dozen cookies on it from behind his back.

I had no idea where he had gotten them.

Cardamom chuckled. "Ricky's gonna kill you. If the Crossroads doesn't first."

Raven picked up a cookie and took a big bite. "Damn, these are good."

Abbi squeezed my hand and leaned around me to Pamela. "He's a good god. He's living in Ordinary and shouldn't be here though."

"Shouldn't is such a strong word," he said. "So are 'good' and 'here.' But I'd love to get out of the rain."

Pamela and her grandfather exchanged looks, then Josie nodded.

"Let's go," Pamela said. "If we want him to leave, I'm sure we can make him leave."

"I love this plan!" Raven said.

He strode to the back of our truck and hopped up into it. "Coming, Bun Bun?"

Abbi leaned in and gave me a big hug. "You're okay," she said fiercely. "All of us are okay. And we can sleep soon. I promise."

Then she released me and jogged back to join Raven.

Elmer gave us a stern look. "I think someone else should drive."

I expected Lula to argue. She didn't like other people touching Silver. But she nodded. "I think so too."

Card raised his hand. "I'll drive. That okay?"

"Yes." Lula pulled me toward the truck. "That's okay."

We piled into the cab. It was a tight fit with the three of us, but Lu tucked herself into my side, her head on my shoulder.

I wrapped my arm around her, holding tight.

The road wasn't smooth, but it didn't stop Lu from closing her eyes. She shivered once, her hand clutching my arm too tightly, and then she relaxed, breathing deeply.

I was fighting to keep my eyes open.

"I got you," Card said. "You can rest, Brogan. I got you."

I fought it still, because I was a stubborn man, but finally the wave of exhaustion was too much. I tumbled and sank down and down.

Card shook me awake. We were in the art deco garage.

I stumbled from the truck, up the stairs and down the hall, Lula just ahead of me, on her feet but weaving a bit.

Lorde made concerned whines and barks, walking beside Lula and pushing her head up under her hand, trying to help support her.

People were talking, maybe even talking to me, asking me things. But I couldn't make out what they were saying, couldn't understand their questions.

Didn't care.

Then there was a bed. Hands pulled away the blankets. I tipped into cool sheets, Lula beside me.

Blankets winged softly over us, and I used the last of my energy to roll toward Lula. I wrapped my arm over her, my bare feet—*where had my boots gone?*—tucked together with hers.

The voices moved away, singing softly, I thought, a song about little stars twinkling.

The lights went out and so did I.

The hunters were trying to be casual. I could see it in their body language, the stiff shoulders, the forced smiles.

I paused in the doorway to the control room to locate the object of their discomfort.

Not object. Objects. Plural.

Specifically, Raven and Cupid sitting at the table,

one looking like a biker with his bald head, diamond earrings, tattoos, and leather vest, the other looking like a man most comfortable in a hoodie, jeans, and sandals.

Both of them were as relaxed as could be, drinking from mugs.

Lula stopped behind me. Usually she would push ahead, eager to take on the problem before me. But she leaned into me instead, her forehead, her full body pressed against me.

Lorde circled our feet, then sat next to us, waiting.

"Gods," Lu mumbled.

I nodded and clasped my hands over her arms wrapped around my waist. "Not done with them yet, I suppose."

She didn't move, just stayed there, holding me, breathing.

Something had changed in her. I didn't know if it was the god magic we'd wielded and how it had marked her. I didn't know if it was the exhaustion from casting the spells and breaking time.

I didn't know if it was finally, finally killing the monster who had attacked us all those years ago.

But now she touched me constantly, turned her face away from the world as if she were done with its light and noise, a weary soldier finally come home from a lifetime on the front lines.

"Want to go back to bed?" I asked.

"Yes." She pushed away, dragging her hand along my back as she came to stand next to me. "But I think I want coffee more."

She strolled into the room, pulling me along with her.

"Morning," Raven called out. "Or should I say afternoon?"

"Is it that late?" I asked.

"Half past three," Elmer noted, taking a seat at the table, but not near the gods who sat opposite each other. "Not that any of us have been up for long."

"I have," Abbi said. "Me and Raven were up all night."

"We all took shifts." Pamela brought a pot of coffee over and set it on a trivet.

"Did you sleep?" Josie carried a tea kettle and a basket with several tea options. She placed those closest to a chair in front of Lula.

Lu sat, and Cardamom came in with mugs and a pile of muffins.

"We did." I sat next to Lu and poured coffee. I offered it to Lu, but she had chosen a black tea.

"Hungry?" Pamela asked. "I have breakfast at the ready, but if you'd rather a lunch I can do that too."

"Breakfast sounds great." My stomach growled and Pamela grinned.

"It'll be out quick. Lu? Anything?"

"Eggs, toast, and fruit, if you have it."

"I do. Be right back. Don't any of you talk about interesting important stuff without me."

Josie dropped down and helped herself to a muffin. "So, what's next?" she asked. "Do we just wait here for another god to attack?"

"We don't," Cupid said pointing between himself

and Raven. "It is very kind of you to have us here, but we do not want to stay long."

"Speak for yourself," Raven said. "These muffins are amazing."

"Not sure our welcome is going to hold out much longer," Elmer said. "The longer you're here, the higher the chance all those other gods and monsters and whatever else you're mixed up with will come knocking on our door."

"Agreed." Cupid turned to us. "So, let's get straight to the interesting important stuff. Lula, Brogan, the next choice you make will change everything. Including your lives and your deaths."

CHAPTER TWENTY

"Dramatic," Raven said. "But not wrong."

He set his mug on the table and tipped his head to both sides trying to loosen sore muscles. "You remember us saying a lost god spell won't cost as much as an existing god spell?" he asked. "The spell cost more than I expected. I think it's because you used it *twice* and the second time you *broke* time. What were you thinking?"

"I was thinking I wanted to see Headwaters dead no matter what it cost," I said around a mouthful of muffin. Raven was right. It was amazing. "Lu?"

"Oh, yeah. Same," she said. "Mix magics? Break time? Good enough if Headwaters got dead enough."

I finished off my coffee and poured another cup. If I was going to hear about my impending death—our impending deaths—I was going to get a couple good cups of joe down me first.

"How much did it cost us?" Lu asked. "What are we going to pay for casting the spells?" She'd decided the same as me, and was sipping tea, her shoulder leaning into mine.

"Ryt's magic, the spell you cast, that's a part of you now," Cupid said. "You can probably tell."

I waited for the feeling of panic, of horror, but I had been through too much for either of those emotions to ping.

"How bad is that?" Elmer asked.

Cupid inhaled, and sort of shook his head. "I don't know. Ryt's power is not mine, that magic is nothing I would create, and it is nothing that has ever been used by an earthbound, god-blessed mortal and a *thrawn*. Mixing it with the watch, which had its own very unusual power…" He rubbed his hand over his bald head.

"It's insanity," Raven said. "Glorious, but insanity."

"Let's just say," Cupid said, "that as far as I can tell, Ryt is correct. If it had torn the spell out of you, you would have exploded. Or worse."

"There's worse?" Josie asked.

"The spell is pressed like a brand into their souls," Cupid explained. "It's also in their flesh, in their DNA. Tearing out a transformation spell by force once it has transformed itself to fit seamlessly into every cell of your body…"

"Okay, yeah," she said. "That's worse."

"So, we're stuck this way?" Lu said. "Our bodies and souls changed by a monster that's dead and trans-formed by a lost god's power which shouldn't even exist anymore?" She shrugged. "At least this time we chose why we were changed."

"And Headwaters is dead," I noted.

Lu flashed a smile that was mostly fang. "Headwaters is very dead."

"But Atë is still out there kicking," Raven said. "So is Mithra, the ass."

"Apep?" Josie asked.

"Big boy over there took care of him." Raven pointed at Cupid. "My hero." He sighed and batted his eyelashes.

Cupid scratched his cheek with his middle finger.

"Back to what you said earlier," I said to Cupid. "We have a choice that will change our lives and deaths?"

"Yes. I can try to separate your souls. To take apart the piece of your soul which was sewn into Lula's and the piece of hers which was sewn into yours. It would be…a delicate procedure. There is no guarantee one or both of you would survive it. But…"

"There's always a but," Raven said.

"But," Cupid went on, ignoring him, "if you wanted me to, I would do so."

"What would even be the advantage to that now?" Lula asked. "It's been so long."

"Atë, right?" Raven asked.

Cupid nodded. "Atë. If I separated your souls, you would no longer be able to use the spells in the book. You would no longer be the hands to hold it and the voice to wield the spells of the gods. You could no longer be used as her tools."

"If we can't be used, she'll just want to kill us," I said.

"She wants to kill you now," Raven agreed, "but

won't. Not so long as she can use you to access the magic ."

"Headwaters is dead," Cupid said. "The monster that changed you is dead. But the monster's master remains."

"We can't kill her using the book. You told us that," I said.

Lu stiffened, then relaxed.

We had tried to use two spells in the book to kill a monster, and it had nearly killed us. How much bigger a spell, how much stronger a magic, would we need to try and kill a god?

"It is not easy to kill a god," Cupid said quietly. "I do not know if you would survive any attempt to do so."

"And there's no guarantee there's a spell in the book that can kill a god," Raven said.

"So, what you're saying, is we can't use the book again? Shouldn't try?" I didn't know if I was relieved or annoyed. The idea that Lu and I alone could wield the power, yes, to kill Headwaters, but also to protect us and those we loved, was a heady thing.

"I'm saying," Raven noted, "that doing it comes with a pretty damn high cost. And I've grown fond of you. Both of you. I'd rather see us find a way to permanently remove Atë from your lives, than see your deaths. The first step for doing that would be to get the book to Ordinary, Oregon, as quickly as possible."

"Breakfast for you," Pamela placed a plate with a generous helping in front of me. "And for you." She settled a plate in front of Lu. "What did I miss?"

"The gods are doing a poor job of talking the

Gauges into giving up wanting to fight Atë and running instead to Oregon as fast as they can," Elmer said.

"I like the sound of that," Pamela said. "Run to fight another day. Or just run to live your lives how you want. What makes Oregon so special?"

"There's a town there," Raven said.

"The gods vacation there," Abbi said. "And there's a magic library that will hide the book."

"There are rules and protections and the Reed daughters," Cupid said, "one of whom can keep any god out of the town no matter what they throw at her."

Pamela whistled. "All right. I like this town. But Oregon? I thought you two were stuck to the Route. That ends in California. It's a long hard day's drive from there to Oregon."

"What happens if you drive off the road?" Cardamom asked.

"The farther we get away from it, the more it hurts," I said. "Well, before. That was before."

"Before?" he asked.

"When I was an earthbound spirit. Before Cupid brought me back."

"You haven't tested it since then?" Josie asked.

I shook my head.

"Locking you to the Route was Atë's doing," Cupid said. "Even killing Headwaters won't have changed that."

"You said we changed," Lu noted. "Not enough to escape that curse?"

"No."

"Let me tackle it," Cardamom said. "I know it was

made with god power, but it's still a curse. There are so many magical ways around a curse, even if it can't be broken."

"You don't need to—" I started.

"I'm going to, so let's just get that out of the way." Determination burned in his eyes. I didn't have to wonder how he'd made his way up the wizard ranks.

"So, is that the plan?" Elmer asked. "You turn and run to Ordinary? Hope you can stash the book before the god catches you?"

"I'll deal with Atë," Cupid said.

"And Mithra," Raven added.

"And Mithra," Cupid agreed.

"And Apep," Raven said.

Cupid glared at him.

"I'm just saying it's three against one, Bo. Bad odds."

"What about taking a stand?" Josie asked.

I shook my head. "Cupid's right. The spells in the book are too strong. I don't know how we'd survive using another one."

"There are other weapons out there," Elmer said. "I'd even wager there's one that can kill a god."

"Oh, there are," Raven said. "Not easy to find, and they come with their own prices to pay, but of course there are."

"How long would it take to find them?" Pamela asked.

"Longer than we have," Lula said. "I say we run."

"Ordinary?" I asked.

"Ordinary," she said. "Bury this book where no one can find it again."

"And Atë and all those other gods?" Elmer asked.

"You are under my protection," Cupid said. "That is no small thing."

"I'll be around," Raven said. "Getting that damn thing to Ordinary is personal."

"We'll help, of course," Elmer said.

"And so will I," Cardamom added. "I know Ricky and the Crossroads will too."

"Me too," Abbi said. "We have a lot of friends now. Isn't it neat?"

I wanted to argue, to tell all these people I didn't want them to risk their lives for us. But looking at the expressions on their faces, I knew I would lose that argument.

"It's more than neat," I said. "It's…" Words failed me, and I gestured helplessly. "Thank you."

The expressions dissolved into smiles.

"Enough of the serious stuff," Pamela said. "Eat. Your eggs are getting cold."

EPILOGUE

Flowers. They were in Lula's red hair, tucked in the vents of the truck, woven in a chain around her wrist. The wild asters we'd created with the god's spell were still fresh and alive, swinging from the rearview mirror, sending the sweet scent of honeysuckle into the air.

She'd found the flowers alongside the road, pulled off, and picked them, holding them to her nose to smell, and laughing at my scowl as she tucked them into my buttonhole, and behind my ear.

"We're running from a god," I reminded her, as the morning sun drenched her in yellow light making her absolutely glow.

"I know. Oregon. I know where we're going."

"You don't seem worried about it." She stood on tiptoe to tuck a second flower in my hair.

"He's dead," she said. "He's dead, Brogan." Her smile was bright, but tears gathered like liquid silver in her eyes.

"Love." I brushed the tears away.

She huffed a laugh. "I'm not sad. I'm not. I'm happy. It's just…I didn't know…for decades…I didn't know if we'd ever find him. If we'd ever…"

"We did," I said. "Broke time for it, have the scars from it. No regretting that from me. Knowing that monster will never take another breath…can never *touch* you again…"

My voice choked on the anger and sorrow rising in my throat. I pushed away the old memories of our attack, focusing instead on the living breathing woman standing in front of me.

"Never," I said. "He's dead and gone. If that's the only thing we get out of this mess, of all the gods and monsters and time and *sorrow*…it's worth it."

She pressed her fingertips gently to the corner of my eyes, wicking away the wetness there.

"I love you, Brogan Gauge."

"I love you, Lula Gauge."

She lifted on her toes again, her hand warm and soft against my face. When we kissed, her lips were honey and wine.

"We just take the next step, right?" she asked softly.

"All we have to do is drive across New Mexico, through Arizona, into California, and then leave the Route and get to Oregon. Easy."

"While gods hunt us," she said.

"Yep," I agreed. "While gods hunt us…and help us," I added a little reluctantly.

She smiled, her eyes crinkling. "Trusting the gods

—*some* of them—" she said, "hasn't been wrong. Cupid gave you back to me."

"I was never gone from you, not for a moment."

"I know. But you're *here*. I can touch you, hear you breathe, hear you laugh."

"You like my laugh?"

"I do. I didn't think we'd have a chance at…this."

"At what? Running from the gods with a spell book of magic so powerful even the two people who should be able to wield it can't?"

"No, not that."

"Having somehow adopted the rabbit in the moon, her angry kitten shadow, and their unending search for cookies?"

The smile grew. "Not that."

"Making friends with monster hunters who should, by all rights be hunting us, a wizard who is on the run from the most powerful wizards in the world, and catching the attention of more gods than I can name?"

"Not even that."

"All right. What didn't you think we'd get a chance at then?"

"Life," she said. "Love."

"Ah, now," I said. "We've always had love. It's the one thing no power—not life, not even death—can take away."

And oh, how she kissed me again.

But now, here in the truck, driving the morning hours away with Abbi perched on her knees looking out the side window, Lorde sleeping contentedly with her head on my foot, and my arm around Lula, I took a moment.

To close my eyes.

To inhale the scent of flowers, dusty road, and crisp, fresh air.

To savor the sensation of the tires thrumming over the old concrete, Lula's hand steady on the wheel.

Lula was humming. That was new too. Singing softly to the country song on the radio.

A song sweetly pining for country roads to take someone home.

And while our road was long, couldn't I almost see the end?

And while our road was dangerous, couldn't I hold a spark of hope that we would survive?

And while we would face the monsters who wanted us dead, powers that wanted to corrupt us, gods who saw us as nothing more than things to be broken and cast aside, wouldn't we still fight?

We would run, yes. Run to Ordinary. But Ordinary wasn't our home. I didn't know if any road could take us home.

But here—right here—in this moment of sunlight, blue sky, ancient plateaus, and plains, this was home.

Because we were together.

Together still, no matter the horrors and pain.

Together still, wearing wildflowers no one would even notice.

Together still, and always home.

THANK YOU FOR READING! You can get an exclusive FREE novella, DUES AND DON'TS as a thank you for hanging out with me. Just go to: www.devon-monk.com and sign up for my newsletter and it's yours!

NOTES AND THANKS

This book wouldn't be nearly as shiny without the help of some talented people.

I'd like to think the amazing artist, Ravven for such a gorgeous cover. I hadn't looked at the art in over a year and didn't realize until after the book was written that Lula and Brogan standing back-to-back would be such an important part of the story. Ravven, you're fabulous!

I'd also like to thank my brilliant copy editor, Sharon Elaine Thompson for turning this book around on such a short deadline. You are so appreciated, my friend!

My deepest gratitude to my husband, Russ, who not only drove Route 66 with me in 11 days (New Mexico was beautiful—and yes, we stopped at the Continental Divide), but has also been so supportive of my writing over all these years. I love you. Also, I want to give a big shout out to my kiddos, Kameron and Mike, Konner and Anna (and Phoebe!). Thank you all for being the best part of my life. I love you all!

To my Patreon readers: Aleta Goin, Alice Hickcox, TJ Thornton, Anne Tisdale, you are wonderful! Thank you SO much for your support!

And to you, my dear readers: thank you for traveling down this magical road with Brogan and Lula, the moon rabbit, and a god or two. I appreciate you all more than you know!

Until next time, happy reading and safe travels!

Pine and Bone - TBA

ORDINARY OREGON MYSTERY

Gorgon with the Wind

For Whom the Spell Tolls

A Seer and Present Danger

HOUSE IMMORTAL

House Immortal

Infinity Bell

Crucible Zero

BROKEN MAGIC

Hell Bent

Stone Cold

Back Lash

Dirty Work

LAS FABLES MYSTERY

Nursery Crimes

WEST HELL MAGIC

Hazard

Spark

AGE OF STEAM

Dead Iron - TBA

Tin Swift - TBA

Cold Copper - TBA

ALLIE BECKSTROM

Magic to the Bone

Magic in the Blood

Magic in the Shadows

Magic on the Storm

Magic at the Gate

Magic on the Hunt

Magic on the Line

Magic without Mercy

Magic for a Price

SHORT FICTION

A Cup of Normal (collection)

One Foolish Joy - TBA

ABOUT THE AUTHOR

Devon Monk is a USA TODAY Bestselling fantasy author. She loves magic, action, hope, and people getting their happily ever afters. So it's no surprise her books are brimming with heart, humor, and people you want to cheer for. She writes short stories (they have magic too!) which can be found in various anthologies and in her collection: *A Cup of Normal*.

She lives happily beneath the rainy skies of Oregon. When not writing, she can be found drinking too much coffee, watching hockey, and knitting silly little toys.

www.ingramcontent.com/pod-product-compliance
Lightning Source LLC
Chambersburg PA
CBHW060548190726
48283CB00003B/919